I0673524

# HIS DISCIPLES IN MOTION

## BOOK FIVE OF THE TERRY REID SERIES

## PATRICK D FERRIS

Print Book ISBN 978-1-9990920-7-8


Published by Patrick D. Ferris – 2021

BOOKS BY PATRICK D. FERRIS:

Larry and Giselle Sports Romance Series

A Gypsy Romance

A Gypsy Engagement

A Gypsy Haunting

*Terry Reid Mysteries*

His Disciples Watch

His Disciples Sleep

His Disciples Deceive

His Disciples Replicate

His Disciples in Motion

*Short Story Collection*

Fragmented Thoughts Random Directions

# CONTENTS

"He urged them to stay humbly on their knees if they wished to remain on this Earth. They quaked with fear, staring at the dark horizon to see if their faith and will could force the sun to rise from the darkness.

The flock kneeled on unyielding earth in the cold and blackness fearing the sun had forsaken them.

They cried out with relief as light finally pierced the blackness, boiling over the horizon, angry and red.

'He' called out, "The Lord put off the 'End of Days' and you are safe, spared once again.""

# A DARK AND STORMY NIGHT

*Dear Terry,*
*    I received an old letter about the real father I never knew. He's off the*
*grid in some cult community that's "Back to nature" in MacLean, Alaska.*
*    I made a decision to boldly go and try to find him,*

*                    Love, Jess*

WET, cold humans toiled in the muddy earth. Buckets of rain howled down upon them as lightning blasted the ground and heavens. Storms of strobe lightning froze them, reluctantly releasing their every motion into a sodden and stuttering grave diggers' dance. They ignored the heavens as they diligently scooped, scraped and clawed in the liquid gumbo, penetrating steadily deeper into the water-filled crater.

At last their shovels stabbed into soft canvas covering what they sought.

After a moment of dread and disgust, they bent to their task, out of sight, heads down in the stinking pit, scratching at the slick muddy package. Reluctant hands wrestled and pushed the bundle up to the surface, slipping and sliding as they fought to escape close contact with it, shoving their prize ahead of them, out of the hole from hell.

Was it blood or treasure they sought?

The leader of the diggers kneeled in the mush, scrubbing rainwater from his eyes before peeling away layers of sodden canvas with shaking hands, nervous to expose its contents. He did as he must do.

There it was!

The diggers leaned over and peered at the prize while a staccato of camera flashes joined light from unsteady headlamps, trembling flashlight beams and punishing lightning strikes, all light sources converging in a blinding flash as if orchestrated, illuminating snaking rivulets of mud sloughing off the exposed… marble-white face.

No one spoke, their shock shutting out the pelting rain that beat against their backs, the ground, the canvas, and the dead man at their feet.

No one heard the rolling thunder overhead, pressing them all down.

They seemed unaware there was someone nestled in the shadows watching while they examined their prize.

A pair of binoculars watched the digging through a slit in the shabby curtains of a long, rough-hewn bunkhouse.

Terry Reid knew a grave digging crew when she saw one.

She peered at the grave robbers, ignoring the sound of rainwater rattling through the eves and the downspouts that led into large rain barrels set at the corners of each building. The windows occasionally rattled with claps of thunder sounding like big guns on a battlefield. They reminded her of her escape from Afghanistan, years ago. The rolling barrage of artillery marching so close to her on the airfield.

Silently, a young girl joined her, whispering, "It was a dark and stormy night…"

Terry lowered her binoculars and narrowed her eyes. "Two years of journalism school for that, Jess?"

"Sorry Auntie. I always wanted to say it."

Terry shook her head and lifted her glasses to resume her vigil. "A writer thing?"

"Yup." The girl looked out at the grave scene with sparkling young eyes. Figures were examining a prone package while rain pounded down in sheets. She squinted as lightning arced over the sky, sometimes close enough to make the hair on her arms crackle with static. She shivered and was glad to be warm and dry. "Holy cow...what the?"

"Shhhh. Look out on the field," Terry whispered.

"Body?"

"Yes."

Jess observed for a full minute. "Who's getting dug up?"

"Not sure. Four diggers and probably a coroner. They had to have been tipped off by someone, which won't go over well. Who knows how many bodies are buried around here."

"Are you going to go out and speak to them, Auntie?"

"Not a chance. I'll bet everyone in this place is sneaking a peek and not saying a word."

"Why *not* say something?"

"I can hear it now—'Oh hi, I was just walking in the rain and noticed you were digging. Is that a body you have there? Imagine my surprise.'"

"Awkward!"

"Go back to bed, Jess. Pretend you didn't hear or see a thing."

"My lips are sealed."

The sound of Jess climbing onto the old, thinly made-up metal army bed was closer to that of hinges on a haunted house door than a place to sleep. It was probably older than both their ages put together. Terry knew these cots well from her police training days. Her mind traveled back twenty years while she continued observing the gruesome unearthing outside.

*Focus!*

Shaking off the old thoughts she adjusted the binoculars to see what they were doing out there. Moving out. They surrounded the stiff, their cold wet hands gripping wet fabric as they stumbled and slid towards their vehicle. One of the diggers clutching a corner of the

3

slimy canvas lost his footing. The canvas escaped his grip, the man fell taking down the person ahead of him allowing the body to escape and splatter down on the mud. It laid there, the pouring rain revealing a naked, chalky white statue. Awkwardly the tired crew recovered the corpse, secured it in the wrappings and headed once again for the Suburban. After slipping and sliding and almost dropping it again, they stuffed it in through the back hatch.

The sodden diggers piled in after. The suburban started up with a puff of exhaust, flash of red taillights and lurched from side-to-side through the mud and potholes of the narrow road and vanished from sight. It would be a long drive sharing a seat with a stiff.

Terry lowered her binoculars.

"Are they done?"

"Yes, done and gone. Just the rain to fill in the hole."

"Ah." Jess whispered, "With the rain barrels full, we'll have fresh water to wash our hair tomorrow. Hopefully there's enough to cover the rations of that suspicious animal fat shampoo, considered a luxury. The Lord doesn't always provide, way out here."

*Sounds ominous.*

Terry whispered to Jess, "The diggers earned their pay tonight. It'll be a quiet and disgusting drive back." No doubt there would be holy hell to pay in the community tomorrow. She was looking forward to it. "There's so much rain pounding the roof you can hardly hear us talk. Saves on running a radio for interference."

"You don't think anyone's listening, do you? Way out here?"

"Count on it! They have a public address system so they can also *listen.*"

"I'm so glad to hear your healthy paranoia." Terry could just make out Jess's toothy grin in the darkness.

Terry climbed into her squeaky metal spring bed nearby. "I'm glad I wasn't in the digging detail out there. What a ghastly night."

Jess was still wide awake. "I'm sorry I got you into this."

"Hey, you're looking up the family tree. The hunt is on. What have you found after a month out here?"

Jess slid up, pulling out her little flashlight. She pulled out the drawer of her night table, flipped it over and pulled out a piece of paper stuck on the bottom and relocated the flashlight to her armpit for better light. She found she needed to hold the letter with both hands because she was a bit shaky.

"While you were away crime fighting, I got this letter with a hand-written note from Cpl. Robert Jenkins, RCMP, Vancouver Cold Case section."

"*Attn: Jessica M. Reid or Constable Theresa Reid, relations of Gloria Reid.*"

"Hey!" Terry interrupted. "I remember Jenkins! He drove the cop car when we were running from the alley in Vancouver, remember?"

"I'd rather not."

"Sorry kid."

"Let me continue... Jenkins wrote, '*Not sure if this is of interest... looking through an old cold case murder and saw the victim pilfered a bundle of mail from the neighborhood including this letter from a 'Miles Vickers' from Washington State to a Gloria Reid.*

*Best regards RJ.*'"

"Pilfered Gloria's mail?" asked Terry.

"I remember who took this mail!!" Jess almost spat on the floor. "Darby Smith, the bag! She claimed to be some pal of ours. When she wasn't mooching off us, she must have been stealing our mail looking for cheques. I hate her! Someone must have bumped her off and she became the cold case Jenkins was looking in to."

Terry smiled at Jess's unusual display of anger. "Easy kiddo. Are you reading your dad's letter or not?"

"Don't rush me. Okay, so the letter starts with,

'*Dear Gloria,*

*I heard you are in the family way and want to help. You have been very difficult to contact by letter or by phone. I do wish to keep news of our wonderful weekend away from my wife as we're almost at the first anniversary of the loss of our daughter and lately her health has not been good. Please reply to me through my cousin, Marvin, and I can send you some money.*

*Sincerely, Miles Vickers.*'"

Terry watched Jess for signs of emotion and saw none. "Sincerely, not love?"

"No. I thought so, too. We never had a phone, and it looks like Darby was stealing our mail, anyway. Life on the edge."

"Miles was fooling around on the side on his ailing wife?"

Jess gave her a withering look.

"Sorry. So, this Miles fellow said he wanted to help while not admitting he was your father."

The tears started to flow. "I know you're right. It's just hard to admit. Maybe I'm reading too much into this. Hope over logic."

"Sorry." Terry hastily added, "How did you track down this Miles fellow?"

"I managed to find the cousin, Marvin Vickers, in Seattle on Face Book. Actually, I found five people called 'Marvin Vickers' and called them all. Two were dead numbers, one was a high school kid, one tried to pick me up and the last one I called said Miles was his uncle."

"And?"

"Seems Miles had an unhappy life. He worked at Boeing, had a daughter and wife, both deceased. Their deaths drove him off the rails. He had drug troubles and eventually joined this cult in Alaska."

"Marvin knew where he went?"

"Somewhat. Apparently, Miles asked Marvin to send his personal effects to Maclean, Alaska, care of 'In Motion'. The package was returned to him undelivered with border duty, so he wasn't completely sure if Miles actually made it or someone out here made sure Miles didn't get it. Marvin thought the package was opened and searched, then returned."

"So, we're at his last *known* location?"

Jess sighed. "As far as we can tell he's around here. Before I left, Amelia dug through this for days. She's a good researcher, you know. She found a reference to him up here. Then the trail went cold and here we are."

"Good job you guys. So, we hang around and listen in for the name 'Miles' in one of these four camps, all get a Disney hug and go home happy?"

"Not quite. It seems most people came here under some alias or nick name—everyone has their story—maybe they're dodging the draft, bill collectors, or the IRS want their souls. Maybe they're hiding from an ex-wife or mafia hit men are looking to bump them off."

"So, this place is 'Foreign Legion' meets Green Acres?"

"Green Acres?" asked Jess.

"Old TV show? About farming... never mind. So, we just wander about and ask for Miles? There's a thousand people up here."

"A needle in a million-acre wilderness haystack," Jess confirmed glumly.

<hr />

IN THE OLD London pub in England, he watched from the side as McBain drink by himself as was his evening custom. The barman made sure McBain got his favourite table in the corner of the Canterbury Pub, so he was easy to spot.

The place wasn't very big with room for about fifty patrons on a busy night and this wasn't a busy night. He suspected he was likely the youngest person in the place. This pub was typical of England these days...a dark, cold and smoky old-folks' home.

As Richard poured back his warm pint of ale, he peered around the room watching for an old face that might be there to haunt him by guarding McBain. Unlikely but he needed to be patient and careful. Follow the plan. McBain was no fool so there would never be a second chance. He slouched in the corner, ignoring the smoke and the noise. Every person in the bar except him seemed to have their heads back, mouths open, laughing uproariously at nothing. They told stories of the good old days, whenever those were. Richard only knew dodgy times with more coming.

This project could put him back on easy street.

Out of the corner of his eye Richard watched McBain creak to his feet and leaned so hard on his cane that it looked like it could break. McBain used his left arm to put on a battered tweed flat cap. After a scan of the money, he'd left on the table, he straightened up, nodded to the barman and stumped through the bar and towards the exit with as much dignity as a drunken man could muster. Richard froze in his chair as McBain paused in the doorway looking over at the men's room. He evidently changed his mind and decided he could make it home without a bathroom break. Or was it a clever way a spy looks for a watcher? McBain leaned into the heavy roughhewn door and stumped out into the darkness.

Once the door banged shut Richard quickly slugged back the last of his beer, spilling some down his phony beard onto his jacket. This beard disguise was a pain in the ass. After flipping three quid on the table, he leaned heavily on his right leg and picked up his crutches. Richard knew anyone from "the Firm" would instantly see through his disguise. That was why he kept his distance from McBain, an old MI6 hand.

Once out the door, Richard made a beeline for the little car he'd stashed behind the pub. Looking both ways he pulled the door open, tossed his crutches in the back and hopped into the driver's seat. He double checked the bag hiding his briefcase. He could smell the gas can. Ready.

He pulled out a highly illegal universal ignition hack fob from his pocket and activated the car's 'start'. E-bay was a godsend, even for criminal endeavours.

Not a bad car at all. An electric car was the best machine to steal for this purpose. In the right hands, they could be so easily changed from an ordinary vehicle into a silent killer. Pity he had to torch it.

Richard pressed the accelerator. The car silently pulled forward. Quickly he spotted McBain's slow deliberate shuffle along the deserted sidewalk. A damaged overhead light crackled on and off like a strobe, giving the solitary walker an eerie long step. On McBain's left there was a series of neatly spaced trees, too large for Richard's car to avoid. Precious moments were lost as he was forced to wait.

He glanced around the roadway for possible witnesses. There were none. This car made barely a sound and he knew McBain was hard of hearing. Guiding the car into position, he resisted turning on his headlights, content for now to shadow the old man. Patience.

His heart skipped a beat when McBain finally moved past the protective row of trees into an open section of sidewalk. Wide open. Richard made a sharp left onto the walk, bounced over the curb edge and accelerated towards McBain's broad back.

---

ON THE OTHER side of London, Terry's mansion guardian Amelia stalked down the dark London alley trying not to trip over trash and drainpipes. Old tall buildings on both sides shielded the narrow alley from light and prying eyes. This was London at its worst and her goal was to get to the other side without being mugged, beaten, or worse. She imagined Jack the Ripper lurking close by, razor sharp knife in his hand, waiting for any warm body to come by. The thought made her shiver.

Keep walking towards the flickering streetlight at the other end. Listen and watch. *I wish I had a flashlight or my knife.*

Her ears amplified every sound she made. Every shadow made her heart skip. What was that? Dripping water or dripping blood?

The air was cold, and the alley smelled of urine, rotten food, and dog poo. Disgusting. She'd have to wash her shoes before she went into the house. Better yet, throw them away.

*Clank.*

What was that? Nothing. Almost out of the alley. Oof! She was shocked by the blow that arched her back. Someone had punched into the small of her spine and now clutched her wool top. The hand jerked her backwards into the black depths of a creepy corner. She heard the clatter of a metal trash can toppling over.

Her impulse was to scream but she held it back, focusing on why she was there. Be calm. No point in thrashing. Wait to meet the person attached to the hand.

---

THE SIDEWALK AHEAD WAS DEAD. A metal gate gently blew back and forth in a bit of a breeze. It made a screeching noise from too little oil and too much rain. There was hardly a parked car to be seen.

Old Mr. McBain leaned hard on his hickory cane as he wobbled towards home after a few pints in his favourite pub. Quite a few. His wife's passing had made his life hard and the pub eased the pain. She endured his strange livelihood and long, unexplained absences and greeted his return without question.

He was lonely in his own thoughts while blankly looking ahead. Pausing, he zipped up the old wool coat she had given him so long ago. It was old and threadbare, not unlike himself.

There were bits of trash swirling around on the walk in front of his feet. He had no way of knowing the car accelerating behind him was bearing down on him. McBain was crushed flat by the silent car he never knew was coming.

---

IN THE ALLEY, Amelia's right foot lashed out in the blackness with a roundhouse boot at whoever was attached to the hand clutching her clothes. A grunt confirmed she'd connected. Her follow-up kick hit someone hard enough for them to groan and release their grip.

Mindless impulse from all her training.

Out of breath, heart pounding, she turned toward the sound of someone falling away from her. She instinctively added another kick which connected where a crotch should be and one more to the head for insurance. Her foot felt odd sinking into real human flesh and bone rather than the sandbags she endlessly kicked at practices.

Jess always coached her to add a few boots to her opponent's head when they were down—and don't run.

"Stop! Stop!" someone shouted to Amelia.

A bright light burst over the alley, showing a man lying at her feet, gasping while trying to roll over. He wheezed and coughed, holding his crotch. Another man walked up to them.

"Okay, Donny?" asked the man.

"I'm ...kinda okay...S'okay..."

Amelia was horrified. "I'm so sorry! Ya surprised me. Isn't this what the exercise is for, Lyle?"

Another man stood nearby, laughing. "This is exactly what it's for. You alright, Donny? I thought you SAS types were tough?"

Donny struggled to get onto one knee, swaying in place. "I am. She caught me off guard, that's all. Couple of pints and I'll be as good as new... erk."

"Your breath tells me you've already had a few pints."

"Yeah... well..."

"Good job Amelia! Did you think we'd let you through the alley scot free?" Lyle was pleased.

"I sneaked along and thought I would make it through. How did I do? Good, huh?"

"You showed good awareness and caution. Good job beating him down after he grabbed you—except..."

"Except?"

"If he'd hit you with a knife, bottle or a club you'd be down or dead."

Amelia swallowed and wiped off sweat with her sleeve. "Sorry Lyle. It's so dark."

"It's all right. That's what this simulation is all about. Self-defence 101 and I'll give you a B-plus."

"What should I have done?"

Donny groaned and struggled to his feet mumbling, "Good kick to the jewels, Amelia. My child rearing days are behind me now."

"I'm so sorry." Amelia was appalled but secretly pleased at the same time.

Lyle reassured her. "Don't worry about Donny. He'll be fine. A few pints and he'll be telling us all about hand-to-hand combat with the IRA."

She nodded.

"Let's talk about this simulation some more. What I like to do is scan the whole area before stepping in. There's only so many places to hide, usually doorways and dumpsters. It's low light but there are shadows. Move to the edges and pause, listen and smell. Be patient. Sometimes you can hear someone breathing or catch the scent of a smoker or their cologne. Jump *them* before they jump *you*."

"Wise words."

"Glide your feet on the ground rather than stepping. Move heel-toe. Use the shadows. Jump *them* before they jump *you*. In alleys, people act like cats and mice—be the cat. Anticipate a move, pause, listen, then pounce. Think cat... Got it, Donny?" Lyle teased.

"Cat... Got it," he nodded foolishly.

"And here's your purse, flashlight and knife."

"Thanks." Amelia slung the purse over her shoulder, shoved the light in her left pocket and carefully slid her knife into its sheath in her right, enjoying the way the light glinted off the blade as she did.

Donny wiped at his bloody nose with the back of his hand and grinned. "A Khukuri knife?"

"Not quite. It's a Khukuri *throwing* knife...it's a smaller, handier version," Amelia corrected.

"What would you do with that little knife if you had a chance?"

In a heartbeat Amelia flipped the deadly little Khukuri knife into her fingers and effortlessly snapped it across the alley. Thwack! It sank into the center of a Guinness beer sign leaning against a dumpster, piercing the plywood.

Amazed, Donny asked, "Where'd you learn that?"

"Friends in low places," she answered, sauntering across the alley to retrieve her knife. "Jane Bond showed me." No need to mention she got them on sale from Karate Mart. Her grandfather would have been proud as he loved a bargain, bless him.

Lyle brought the evening to a close. "Shows over. You need to get home and get some shuteye. School tomorrow."

"Sure. G'night," she said, smiling at him.

She'd only met Donny twice, but she did enjoy his company and wonderful Irish drawl. Kicking in Donny's nether regions hadn't helped her chances of getting a date, tonight.

Damn.

## 2

---

# BEING FOLLOWED

Richard's car bounced over McBain, leaving him on the sidewalk like an anonymous family pet, crushed and abandoned.

Serves him right!

Richard pushed the switch for the headlights and noticed both had been broken by the impact—as were his turn signal lights. No matter. Avoiding main streets, he dodged slowly around his route grateful for the odd working overhead light.

He saw no one.

His sense of elation vanished as he hoped and prayed the police weren't coming to McBain's aid. With any luck at all the elderly folks in the neighborhood wouldn't find anything until daylight.

It was a left turn on Keller Street that led to the grimy underpass below the motorway. He slipped into a parking place next to a burnt-out car he'd previously scouted out. It was a notorious dumping ground for stolen vehicles, drug transactions and a few bodies but usually not until later in the night.

He came to a stop when his bumper crunched into the heavy concrete barrier. Richard glanced into the rear-view mirror, turned the car off and pocketed the fob. After rescuing his crutches and the bag with his briefcase in it from the vehicle he yanked a small plastic gas can out from behind the seat. One more peek around.

The plastic can's gas cap came off easily and he splashed it over the seats and floor of the little car. His lighter set it aflame. He paused to watch the smoke turn to flame engulfing the car's interior, tires, under the bonnet and motor compartment. The batteries made sure this was a hot one and would melt the aluminum and carbon fiber body.

This was such a sketchy area so fire trucks wouldn't come around here without police protection which required coordination. He knew fireman feared car battery flames and its noxious smoke and would stay way back to leave electric cars to burn themselves out. Hopefully all evidence would be nothing but a molten cinder.

He moved with his crutches as fast as he could, heading for the nearby tube station and his ride home. Part one of his plan was done.

---

AMELIA SAT in the tube car seat still shaking from the evening's assault simulation. She felt a sense of joy, fear and failure at how it went. Poor Donny took a beating from her which she felt bad about.

It crossed her mind that Lyle and Donny might try to follow her to extend the simulation. Those buggers would get a laugh out of that! Not on me!

The subway train lurched and screeched to a sudden stop. She had to make a quick decision. She leapt up and out the door, barely getting through, then ran up the stairs and hopped into another subway train going the opposite way. She snickered, thinking of Lyle and Donny trying to catch her. Looks like she had this car all to herself which made her a bit nervous, this late at night. Luckily, she had her knife and hoped she didn't have to explain it to a copper, again. Her cover story was a tearful museum project about Ghurkhas and her grandfather.

Family heirloom.

She surreptitiously glanced around the car, making note of a homeless man sleeping to her far right. There was a smell of fresh paint from the latest graffiti above her, *"The King Stinx!"*. Someone had abandoned a greasy fish and chips paper bag on the aisle floor. A middle-aged man with a beard hobbling along on crutches entered the car. He sat at the far end, looking away.

Lyle dressed up? She considered running by and yanking his phony beard off. What if it wasn't Lyle? That would be awkward.

She waited until the last second and jumped out, dashing across the station to the car she really wanted. Digging around her school bag she pulled out a wide blue hat, stuffed it on and paused to see if anyone followed her.

Surprise, surprise—along came the bearded man on crutches again. He settled at the end of this car, same as in the last car. He'd have had to move danged fast, since she'd run to get here. She'd watch this guy closely.

Amelia made one more hat and train switch to ditch the bearded man. It had to be Lyle, though this guy seemed oddly shorter and pretty fast for crutches. Didn't matter. Her kicks would keep him hobbling for a while.

---

In Alaska Terry considered their dilemma. "If we're going to locate your dad, if he's up here, we can narrow it down to older men which are about a third of this operation. Got a list?"

"I doubt there's a real, master list of names of actual people. There wouldn't be any need for it." Jess returned the letter to its hiding place then turned off the flashlight.

"I wonder..." said Terry aloud.

"What?"

"Only real names get the real money. They were particular about our names so they could get our dough, weren't they? You won't get that with phony names."

"Could there be a real list out here?"

"Depends if they have computers or not. Too rustic."

"Follow the powerlines, if there are any."

"They carry this back to the earth thing way too far. No cell or internet service, electricity or modern vehicles. Their idea of medical is herbs and prayer."

"Ah, God will heal—which must be why there are bodies scattered about," added Terry.

"Do you think there's more?"

"Probably."

"Natural and... unnatural?"

"The Enforcer Angels make sure us simple folk don't escape. They don't just make us stay home from school if we're bad."

"Don't you think the term 'Angel Enforcer' has an ironic twist?"

"Yes."

"Are the Angels hired knuckle-draggers or just folks they had around?" asked Terry. "Maybe the ruling Angel bosses pulled them out because they were shitty farmers."

"Shh, Aunty. No swearing around here."

"Sorry. Jess. Ah..., you didn't sign over all your money, did you, Jess?"

"No. They didn't get all my worldly goods, 'cause I don't have any. I claimed I was a penniless runaway. They're good with that; I'm a cheap labourer and child bearer. You sign over anything?"

"Nope. I had bogus I.D. papers made by Gomez. I told the border 'Motion' greeters that I just spent all my money on a new house, and it burned down in a lover's spat. No insurance and my no-good husband vanished so I'm footloose and fancy free. Finding the Lord and all that."

"Seems like an unduly complex back story, Auntie."

"They liked the drama. I named myself Gina Gospel," said Terry proudly.

"You named yourself after the ex-head of the CIA? You're betting they won't know Gina Gospel is supposed to be cooling her heels in a cell in Guantanamo Bay?"

"Yes, well, more than one person can have the same name."

"Why not a Pam Jones or something?"

"Do I look like a Pam?"

"I'm not sure what a Pam is supposed to look like," Jess grumbled.

"Besides, I was hot on your trail. No time to conjure up anything better. Still, I'm sure they will try and check me out. It'll be a dead end if they try."

"So what if I have a fake name? I got the impression they didn't care who you were just so long as they got your strong back and your money. Even the people here seem to operate under aliases and nick names or just 'citizen'."

"And you used the name...?"

"Um... Greta... Garbo."

Terry laughed so hard she snorted. "The old-time movie star! Awesome!"

Jess was a little embarrassed and changed the subject. "Yes, well... How did you locate this place?"

"Amelia told me about your letter, I followed you to Maclean, and saw there were four communities nearby."

"You chose the 'East' community? Why east?"

"East was first alphabetically. You have an orderly mind and would start searching at the beginning," Terry pointed out.

"Ah."

"'The Motion' didn't supply transport for me so I left Maclean, hitchhiked to this East place and walked the last couple of miles to get in here and beat the rain."

"Hitchhiked?" asked Jess incredulously.

"Yes. An old farm couple picked me up. They said I looked like one of those loopy commune kids."

"We do! Did you come in the main gate?"

"It was dark, so I crawled through. Nobody saw me."

"Wasn't there a sentry?"

"Yup, went around him. He was sleeping."

"How'd you find me?"

"I went to their main office, registered and asked to room with someone. They showed me a paper list of clearly bogus names and I saw 'Greta Garbo', your favourite old actress."

"Am I that predictable?" Jess grumped unhappily.

"It's not a bad thing."

"Time for shuteye, Auntie. They get us up early."

"Early? I just got here. Don't I get time to acclimatize? The community tour with tea and donuts with little colored sprinkles?" pouted Terry.

"Nope. Up at five forty-five for a prayer in the square, then six-sharp for a bowl of gruel and brown water they claim is coffee and then it's off to the fields we go. Make sure you use the bathroom. Outhouses are lined up on the right, on the edge of the sheep field."

"Sounds cruel. What if I sleep in and ignore the wake-up call?"

"A goon 'angel' will come and get you."

"Will he be cute?"

"Nope. Ugly and nasty."

"Ah. Terrible hotel. I'm giving this place a shitty review."

"And here we are, trapped in Stalag Nine while Amelia is back in London in our awesome English Manor."

"Priorities. We're on the hunt for your dear old Dad."

---

RICHARD GOT out of the tube station at midnight. He made a quick visit to the disgusting subway toilets. His beard was now hidden in the briefcase along with folding crutches. The stolen car was probably a pile of ashes. He now looked like any other office worker returning from a late-night shift. There wasn't a video camera or witness that could identify him.

He did wonder if that girl on the first tube car saw him. Didn't matter. All she saw was a disguised stranger.

There wasn't much time for sleep, and he had to be at work early tomorrow. He had big shoes to fill... McBain's!

AMELIA'S PHONE alarm woke her up at nine a.m. As her eyes opened, she looked up and saw the old frescoed painting on the ceiling in her room featuring hounds, horses, and a fox hunt.

The beautiful room chandelier glinted in the sun that cascaded through the large side window that featured a stained-glass caricature of prince something-or-another's coronation.

Another day in this lovely mansion.

The canopied bed was her favourite touch. The walls matched the pattern of her bed spread. Her pillows were handmade from the feathery down of a flock from some unfortunate geese. Poor things.

She laid awake, dreamily imagining Jess and Terry living wild and free in Alaska, roasting marshmallows around a campfire under the stars, serenaded by handsome cowboys with harmonicas and guitars. What a life! Communing with nature, eating fresh caught trout and venison every day after working in fields of flowers in a friendly community of smiling settlers.

Those two had it so good!

On the other hand, here she was living in Phillimore House, a London luxury mansion, all by herself. It was a lovely nine-bedroom, eight-bath abode. A year ago, she was stuck in a one room domestic quarters and now she was lord and master of this magnificent place. Terry called her the Senior Supervisor of the Manor.

Time to get up. No more daydreaming. It was another day to learn about criminology.

Terry and Jess convinced her to live with them and go back to school to expand her horizons. All the cloak and dagger stuff with the Reids whet her appetite for the strange and unexpected. Everything else would be a bore.

Terry suggested she sign up for martial arts, as well, which she did. Friendly bone crushing. The Taekwondo club initially treated her like an outcast, a female, but her warrior spirit won them over. They soon enjoyed beating each other up with a smile.

She whiled away her empty evenings by practicing throwing knives in their basement range. Amelia made a note to keep both of those activities off any future resume.

Maybe she should get a date instead.

Amelia shook knife throwing thoughts out of her mind. After a quick shower she dressed for another day at school, which she looked forward to. She needed to hustle if she was to get to the subway and get on to school.

Today was 'Criminology 101 - Urban' or 'Crime1' as taught by old Mr. McBain, a treasure trove of old Scotland Yard stories. He was frail but funny. His wrinkled, scarred face and hands must have had a dangerous life. This week's topic was tailing and being tailed, so she tried out more of his techniques. It became an old habit after living with the Reids anyway.

They'd both told her to be calm, blend in, go with the flow, be invisible, add a hat or pull a coat inside out to throw them off, stay in shadows, and never run unless bullets were flying.

She practiced her school course disguises constantly. Her bag contained a pair of cheap, ugly eyeglasses, two different colored hats, both reversible, a gray raincoat with a beige flip side and hood and two different colored small umbrellas. There was make up for quick red or blue lips and white pancake skin powder as well. From school-girl to bizarre street person.

Terry was a wealth of information on this and Amelia was looking forward to her return.

She arrived at school in time to grab a coffee, walk in the door and sit down. Maybe she could share the story of the bearded man with crutches with old Mr. McBain and the class. They'd laugh.

Sitting with her twenty classmates she waited and wondered when Mr. McBain would appear. He was usually punctual. He gently chided her for being late three weeks ago. "Late night date Miss Pun?" That had embarrassed her and spurred her on to getting to school on time.

She absently looked around at the hall they were cooped up in. A drop of rainwater dripped onto her desk. The hall was elderly with water stains spreading out on the sculpted vaulted ceiling. Rumour had it the plan was to fix the leaks on next year's budget, but she'd also heard they'd said that last year too. Her hand caught a chip out of the rough desktop she sat in, reminding her the room furniture was just cheap, beat and nasty. College ambience.

Her bored classmate's chit-chatted about real and imagined conspiracies and last night's MI6 TV police show. The TV stars were so good looking and they always seem to know what was going to happen. The marvels of television. Tiffany led the discussion.

Amelia thought Tiffany and about half her class were considering show business after they graduated. Dumb rich kids. The rest fancied law enforcement but would end up as night shift security in some obscure government building or shopping center, throwing out drunks or cleaning up puke on the floor.

Eventually a stranger appeared in front of them and cleared his throat. The students stopped speaking and sat back down. Standing in front of the class was the bearded man with crutches from the subway!

---

IT WASN'T the best sleep Terry ever had. The creaking springs of her old iron mattress reminded her of her army and cop training days. The springs were hard and long, bringing back thoughts of joy, tears and blood. Was that a spider nibbling at her toes? Jess snored like a cow, obviously tired from a hard day's work. Terry then thought of Dean, her past lover, and gently slipped into dreamland.

A disembodied metallic voice called out, "Now hear this!"

Terry and Jess were rudely awakened by a loudspeaker blaring a scripture at five forty-five.

*"But watch yourselves lest your hearts be weighed down with dissipation and drunkenness and cares of this life, and that day come upon you suddenly like a trap. For it will come upon all who dwell on the face of the whole earth. But stay awake at all times, praying you may have strength to escape all these things that are going to take place, and to stand before the Son of Man.*

*Remember: you are special and here to serve the Lord's purpose. Only trust us and our Lord."*

"Rise and shine, Aunty."

With a groan of defeat, Terry's eyes popped open. No use pretending. "I just got to sleep. Is this like the MASH TV show? This mattress is as old as I am. Do they wash these sleeping bags ever?"

"Possibly."

"Smells like farts, b.o., and bad breath."

"You're getting soft, Auntie. I thought you army types slept on a bed of rocks, ate grubs and tree bark, and marched fifty miles a day in your bare feet on broken glass."

Terry sat up, looking mildly indignant. "That's the God's truth but, I *am* getting old."

"Time to get up you poor old dear."

Terry stretched, then slid off her bed to stand on the rude board floor, rubbing the sleep from her eyes. How many strangers had stood in this exact spot over the past decades? Dressing didn't take long in the drab, chilly bunkhouse. It was tiny so they took turns at the chipped white cold-water basin to scrub their hands and faces by the feeble light coming through the cracked window. With one hard shake, the old sleeping bags would take on the appearance of rude duvets—at least that seemed to be the idea. It didn't translate well; in fact, it didn't translate at all. They were still thin, beat up sleeping bags covering tortuous metal beds.

"How do they heat these rooms in winter? Warmed up rocks?"

Jess shrugged. "Beats me. We'll be gone by then."

Terry watched Jess hide a picture of her mom and a book under her mattress. "Hiding your stuff? Do they snoop in here?"

Jess nodded.

Terry was last out of the room and pulled the door closed. No lock. She shoved a splinter of wood in the crack of the door. *We'll find out if this gets opened while we're gone.*

She made a quick trip to the smelly, cold seats of the outhouse. It was filled with other women who looked unhappy with puffy red eyes and handled squalling children.

"Where do you wash your hands, afterwards?"

"A puddle?" Jess shrugged and smiled. "A 'ten-holer' outhouse for your convenience. We go over to that square, in front of the pulpit and cross."

Terry glanced around. "I wonder how they scored these old army camps. Maybe left over from the cold war days?"

"Could be. I see some military type signs painted over here and there. 'No Urinating Here', 'VD Kills' and 'Uncle Sam Needs You!'."

"Classy."

"This place is pretty run down. Anything special about this place?"

"It has a defensible entrance, a river nearby for water, and power. This marching square with a flagpole is classic."

"That's comforting."

"Reminds me of my army days. 'Square bashing' we called it. Marching around while someone swore at us. Heartwarming. Brings a tear to my eye." She hammed it up, dabbing pretend tears with her hand.

They both followed directions from the Angels who waved their long staffs and stood waiting for the remaining people to dribble in. Everyone looked drab, cold and tired. Some couples dragged along a few sleepy, bawling kids.

With narrowed eyes, Terry carefully surveyed the drab buildings surrounding the dirt square. Deep, unmowed grass mixed with dandelions and wild daisies with a few new scrub trees trying to exist in a busy area of the square's foot traffic. A forlorn flagpole stood in the middle sporting a ragged stars and stripes. It was all a cross between Hogan's Heroes and the family version of Bridge over the River Kwai.

She noticed there was a system to the layout of the dwellings. Families had their own tiny homes, usually a flat-roofed log cabin style. The 'supervisory' crowd had bigger, nicer homes on the periphery. One home looked like it had been converted into a barracks, probably for the 'Angels'.

Terry saw a few oversized livestock barns on the edge of the community, near the fields. The tool shed was near the entrance. There were piles of split wood everywhere, enough to supply all the stoves in the huts and buildings.

There were large fields of crops she could see. They were colors of green, brown and yellow. She was too much of a city slicker to know what varieties they were. They did look pretty as they waved in the morning's gentle breeze.

Two cookhouses stood in the center of the community—long wood-slab buildings with three crooked, rusty chimneys poking out. Jess told her one was the cafeteria for the "Citizens", which became the school after meals were completed, and had a rudimentary laundry on the end. The second long cookhouse building was for the staff and was clearly better supplied and off limits to the citizens unless they worked there. Someone had a good start on cementing stones up the sides of this building.

Their last stand, "hold out" bunker.

She was positive the "boss buildings" had electric lights inside. Unmistakable. She didn't hear a diesel generator anywhere close. Had to be underground cables. Did God or Uncle Sam supply solar or a water turbine from a nearby little dam? Might be a good one to investigate.

The last item she noticed before the sermon started was the long stone wall snaking around the community. Five years of five crews, twelve hours a day, picking rocks generated tons of free—just the right price—solid building material. The surrounding wall now reached a height that could easily keep out all but the most determined vehicles and would no doubt be bullet proof.

Big fences were excellent guards against intrusive outsiders.

And also trapped folks inside.

---

MILTON HOBSON GAZED UNHAPPILY at the huge Alaska map on the wall. His brother Randolph Hobson sat across the desk from him.

Milton said, "Unless we finish homesteading that Alaskan land by next year, we won't get the oil rights and enough cash to seize this state. These communities must be self-supporting like the management units."

Randolph shook his head. "Why don't we bring in some real equipment, make the homestead deadlines and pocket the cash? We have promising oil and industrial projects all over the continent."

"Aren't you bored with spending money? *I* am. It's time to unleash the buying power of our hidden trillions!" Milton looked at him angrily. "We're here to do God's work for the "Council of Disciples", not just to make oil money. Here's a chance to get and keep the finances and make use of our communities' free labor to take over Alaska. We'll have our own country—almost as large as continental America."

"A takeover? The government isn't going to just roll over and let this happen."

"We'll try a legal takeover from the top, starting with Governor Fairfield. He thinks like us and wants to get out from under Washington's military government. We get him to cook up some emergency and take over, giving it all a veneer of legality."

"Governor Fairfield? Can that knucklehead be trusted? Remember when they caught the CEO of the Bristol Creek Alaskan Pebble Gold Mine hot on Zoom? He was bragging to some phony investor how he had the governor in his pocket, bought and paid for. That mine was busted in a week."

"Easy Randolph. That was a clumsy first try. We've spent more time with Governor Fairfield than Dunleavy, and Fairfield has a lot more to lose. The dossier we've worked up on his personal life could send him to prison for the rest of his natural life."

Randolph shuddered to himself. *Who is this evil man I call my brother?* He continued. "Will Canada allow American troops through their territory to attack us?"

"Still working out the kinks on that. Might be prickly…"

"American troops could fly in."

Milton seized on his statement. "Nope! Runways dug up." He swept his hand north of Alaska. "There's no way the Russians will tolerate America flooding troops in next to their borders."

"True…"

"We build up our assets and let Governor Fairfield declare independence. The National Guard from the communities do a few parades, take over a few coastal cities; we declare ourselves the Republic of Alaska and we're done."

Randolph smiled. "Since they won't let us make America a Revisionist country then we'll liberate it ourselves, a bit at a time, just like George Washington did by attacking the Brits. A home for us at last."

"No more hiding."

They clinked glasses. "To the Council of Disciples!"

Deep down Randolph shuddered at Milton's latest crazy scheme. He set his glass down. "This is a lot of work for a small return, but we need to start somewhere."

Milton sighed. "It's a good work-around. My sources tell me the military government has big changes in the works—officially calling it, 'Good Government Waiting for Good Leaders.' Unofficially they're calling it 'Taking government back from the bloody billionaires. I'm insulted—I'm a trillionaire; you're a trillionaire. I call it *stealing it* from the trillionaires."

"How dare they! We built this country!" Randolph scoffed, comfortable again in sharing Milton's disdain. "*We* built this country; *we* paid for that military."

"To be fair the military did what our government asked." Milton's eyes were twinkling with humor now.

Randolph added with a smirk, "After we told them what we wanted."

They both snickered. Milton refilled their glasses and said, "True. Getting controlling interest in Mideast Oil hasn't hurt one bit." Raising his glass to Randolph he proclaimed, "Power is our calling, not mere money."

They sipped their wine in comfortable silence.

## 3

# SQUARE BASHING

Lionel Garson the Second stood shivering at his high pulpit at the front of the square awaiting his flock to gather. He was the community Speaker from God and supervisor of all he surveyed. Impatiently he directed his two Enforcer Angels to speed up the dawdling group to line up in the square.

It was always the same...some came early and stood annoyed while others arrived at the last minute. He'd tried starting on time, regardless of their attendance to embarrass the stragglers into getting here early but it never worked. He suspected some deliberately came later to miss his sermon.

The Angels were sent to deal with them. More often than not, they would be leaving the community on foot with only the clothes on their backs.

He saw Angel Jeb in his brown overalls waving his long wooden staff shouting, "Hurry up! Four lines!"

Similarly dressed, Angel Isaac waved his staff at a slow-moving pair on the left. "Line up on these dirt marks, you! Move it."

TERRY WHISPERED, "Who are these guys with staffs and Friar Tuck outfits? Is this a Robin Hood play and we missed getting the show program?"

Jess murmured back, "Easy. We are here, undercover, remember? Dear old Dad? Eyes on target."

"Got it. I am being nice...but if he whacks me..."

"Shhh..."

Terry held her breath, doing as she was told. Slowly she moved her eyeballs to observe the people in the square. They were all ages, a few families and a lot of single people. All were skinny, tired and compliant, their eyes vacant as they loitered in place.

She thought, work them hard, feed them a little, march them around and they'll do as their told...just like the military has done since medieval days. At least they gave you a spear or a club back then.

---

FINALLY, everyone was assembled. Lionel stood tall, imperially surveying his flock. The community had accumulated almost two-hundred and fifty people of all ages. It was essential to their plan that this community, as well as the three others, become a homogenous group doing as they are told.

He fondled the ancient, cold metal microphone, fiddled with the on-off switch thumbing it twice to make sure it worked this time. Without bothering to say 'test' or 'good morning' or any other pleasantries he belted out the chosen scriptures, looking out onto the sea of faces before him. With conviction he impassioned, *"Because He loves each of us so much, God assigns angels for our protection. No matter who you are, how low you may feel in life, God doesn't discriminate who gets angels to watch over them. Instead, He tells others to "not despise" one another. In addition, the angels have direct access to God and are a helpful communication liaison between heaven and earth.*

*"As you leave for nourishment be sure and thank angels Isaac and Jebediah for their protection.*

*"Remember: you are special and here to serve the Lords purpose. Only trust us and our Lord."*

*"Bow your heads in prayer..."*

Lionel took a breath and looked out into the crowd hoping for any sign of enlightenment or even one joyful grin. He saw nothing but tired, blank faces looking forward to breakfast, such as theirs was.

Expressionless silence. It was disheartening but not unexpected. He wasn't there for their acceptance.

———

TERRY WATCHED Lionel finished speaking then stand back as if he'd accomplished something wonderful. His two 'Angel' henchmen peered through the crowd watching for someone not paying attention or simply sleeping on their feet. Their eyes passed over her uncomfortably. She leaned closer to Jess and muttered, "I think the Angels are jerks."

"Shhh. Best hustle to breakfast. There isn't enough food to go around. Keeps us on our toes, apparently."

Upon a terse dismissal they dashed for breakfast, arriving at the food building in the first quarter of the queue. The long drab building reminded Terry of a prison camp minus the barbed wire set up in the middle of 'Nowhere Alaska'.

They shuffled along as the subdued but orderly chow line inched forward. Nobody spoke except for a few small children. It was cold here, apart from the area around the cook ovens where the cooks bathed in sweat as they shoveled out servings. Someone handed her a cold, chipped white metal bowl, cup and tin spoon. She moved along until she faced a tired man about her age standing across from her. Wordlessly he plopped a spoon of something whitish...possibly watery porridge...into her bowl—*Splat.*

"Please sir, I want more," she told him in a sing-song voice before smiling at him.

He didn't return her smile or make eye contact.

Jess poked her side with her spoon. "Hey."

She turned to Jess and grumbled under her breath, "This is like Oliver Twist without the singing and dancing."

Jess ignored her.

"And where's the sugar and milk?"

Jess's blank look stifled her next question.

Someone down the line called out politely, "Move along. Next!"

She moved along. A young girl slopped "coffee" into her chipped mug, but it barely smelled like it. There were no condiments for it, either.

She made another sidestep to the next sweating server. This woman pulled a bun from the bin in front of her, crudely ripped in half and casually plunked it onto Terry's tray. It looked as if the flour had been locally ground to a rough state and baked some days ago. This was as natural as it got and now stale as a log. She didn't try for butter.

Was something squirming in this bun? Her stomach gave out a gurgle.

She stood with her breakfast, puzzled for a minute, wondering where Jess had gone. The big room was buzzing with people hurrying everywhere.

Jess waved her over to the end of a big, rough-hewn table and long bench. There seemed to be a pecking order for seating. The important looking folks all sat at one table nearest the door, singles at another and families on any ends they could find. Everyone had an urgency and efficiency to eating.

Any prayers were done at fast forward.

She sat down and listened. Heads bowed down to the task at hand, the sound of metal spoons scratching out every morsel of the suspicious porridge in the metal bowls. It sounded like fingernails on the rusty bars of a cell. A few licked the bowls eyeing their neighbors, daring them to call them on it.

Nobody dared to ask for seconds.

Not a chatty bunch this morning. The others weren't wasting their breath or time until they finished. Bad experience?

She looked down at her bowl speculating about what was in there.

She'd had worse. It could have been some type of barley cereal watered down like soup. Was it too much to ask for a few raisins?

Back to the intruder in her bun. Was that a green worm?

In other times or places she was sure Jess could have taken a picture of it with her phone and look up its type on the internet and inform her, 'it's an eight-toed squirmus-yuckus, Auntie'. *Of course,* it was.

Terry pushed the wormy bun over to the edge of her tray. Maybe it could wriggle itself to the edge of the table and fall off on its own. She tried out the mush and found it 'not terrible' if that was a rating. She'd been living the good life for too long. Getting soft.

The door boomed open and everyone held their breath. Enforcer Angels Jeb and Isaac stomped through the entrance. It became so very quiet.

Without pause, the Angels rudely barged to the front of the line-up. People at the tables resumed the noise of breakfast. The sound of spoons in bowls sped up and some people began to bumble towards the exits. Have the wolves arrived? Frightened chickens began scattering from the hen house.

She watched as the two Angels gave the cook an evil eye and got four times as much as anyone else had received. This left those remaining in the line with little or nothing. Empty bowls and shrugs 'sorry' from the cooks. No one protested to the Angel Enforcers.

Terry whispered, "I wondered why those two looked so well fed."

Jess whispered back, "Normally supervisory people get fed at another building with much better chow than we get. They come here to keep order over us peons."

"Those guys keep order? Folks here are skin and bones and dead tired. How much pushback could there be?"

"We had a food fight. There was a huge screaming match when they ran out of food the second day I got here. The Angel goons ran in, staff clubs swinging. It took half the day to clean up and resume field work."

"Good lord."

"Shh! They're coming to sit here."

Angels Jeb and Isaac imperiously came over and plunked them-selves between a rapidly clearing group on one end of the table with Terry and Jess on the other. The benches creaked with their weight as they plopped down, grinning. They laid their thick wooden staffs on the tabletop the way a person might place a rifle in a Dodge City saloon. *I dare you to touch it, greenhorn.*

They were beefy, big and forbidding with prison tattoos to match.

Jess elbowed Terry, gesturing her to finish eating and leave. Her eyes ordered Terry to go, as best they could without words. To her horror Terry struck up a conversation with the two Angels, ignoring Jess's warning expression.

"Nice looking wooden staff's there, gents. Nice knife work. Did you make them yourselves?"

They stopped eating and stared at her like a pair of rabid watch dogs.

"Why's that?" Jeb spoke as if his words should scare her to the bone.

Jess kicked Terry under the table.

Terry wasn't the least intimidated. "Good workmanship. Hickory or elm?"

"How would I know?" Jeb said gruffly, surprised at her boldness.

"Looks good enough for Gandalf."

Jeb looked blank, clearly baffled. "Gandalf? Someone new?"

Terry guessed they weren't big literary fans while Jess suppressed a grin.

Isaac gestured to her plate. "Doing anything with them breakfast buns?"

"Want 'em?" Terry smiled amiably, snatching Jess's away from her hand before she got a bite and handed both over to the tatted-up goons.

Jess kicked her harder this time.

Surprised at the lack of resistance the goons shoved the buns into their faces without taking their eyes off her and made a point of chewing like they just conquered something or someone.

She barely kept a straight face as she imagined the worms

squirming in their mouths. Squirmus-yuckus? "We gotta go…cows to milk or something." Terry stood and towed Jess out of the building.

Jess spoke when they were past the door. "What were you doing? Those guys are the guards!"

"I'm finding out who they are. Non-military types, tatt's and accents of low-level criminals from the LA area. Soft hands with scars. Renta-goons. Beatings on request."

"Why'd you give them our buns? I was hungry."

"That wasn't spinach in those buns…green wiggly worms!"

Jess made a stricken face and stuck out her tongue. "Worms? Bleh!"

Terry nodded toward the cookhouse window. "Check out Moe and Curley in there yukking it up, eating our wormy buns."

"Eew! That *is* funny."

As she looked through the window the two enforcers were eating the buggy buns and laughing, looking defiantly around the room.

"You just interviewed them to see who's guarding the place?"

"Yes. I wanted to see if we are being guarded or guided."

"What's the difference?"

Terry thought about it. "Guards use guns and guides use sticks."

"Comforting."

"They're low-level guards, Angel Enforcers, to protect us, so to speak. The guy at the pulpit is probably a spokesman for the camp commandant, whoever he is."

Jess side glanced her suspiciously. "You're scouting this place out."

"Damn rights. Seeing who's got the keys to the jail."

"Ah." Jess changed the subject. "Look—see that guy over there? That's where we go for work. Follow him to the stone boat."

"A boat? Where's the water?"

"There's no water."

"So, what are we doing?"

"Picking rocks."

"Ah. Look, there's a pretty rock over there. I pick that one. I like this job."

"Very funny. Follow me."

It was the beginning of a lovely sunny day.

THE MACLEAN ALASKA Police Office was not a happy place. An inert grey body stretched out on a makeshift morgue table in Coroner Dr. Rick Forest's make-shift office. The scent of formaldehyde and death drifted out the door, enveloping the entire space. It was an inconvenient situation.

Sheriff Abe Kelly squawked from the safety of his office, "Aw, Rick! I *already* looked over that body when you brought it in."

Coroner Dr. Rick Forest shot back, "Come do your job! We spent hours digging it out of a field in the pouring rain."

No reply from the sheriff.

Discouraged, Rick took a deep breath. He was a big old guy and been the town veterinarian for forty years—used to pushing around big animals so nobody wanted to razz him too much and risk getting a bone crushing poke in the face. A few of them still had bruises from playing hockey with him.

The only reason he'd stood for the coroner's job was it had looked interesting and his colleagues had dared him to. "Here's a chance to find out how human bodies work, Rick. They aren't cows, horses or parakeets," they'd teased.

He of course, applied and, of course, got the job.

He'd now been the part time coroner for ten years. He had witnessed many strange, sad and terrible things. Be careful what you wish for.

He smiled with satisfaction because he knew Sheriff Abe had to cave or Rick would threaten to quit. Abe would have to break his meagre budget and fly in a real coroner from Fairbanks. A holiday in Maclean.

Sheriff Abe stomped in. "You're killing me, Rick—this place stinks. Get rid of this body, right now!"

Rick shut him up by pulling back the sheet, exposing a white corpse of the old man. "Here."

The sullen sheriff reluctantly looked at the naked body, as white as marble, shriveled and sporting a large official tag tied to the left toe.

Abe muttered the obvious, "Probably old Samuel M. Bemon. They didn't want him identified. Your point?"

"He's been beaten to a pulp, especially his face. Look here, here and here. Broken bones there and there, all done before a secret burial."

Abe shrugged it off. "You guys did that to him digging him up. Shoulda waited for daylight. Sign the death certificate and get rid of him. He's stinking up the place."

"A medical examiner needs to do an official autopsy on him!"

"*You* do it! That's why you get the big bucks," Abe scoffed. "Besides, why would I pay to fly in a real doc, feed and water him and fly him back for a naturally dead old hermit living out in one of those damned communities?"

"Samuel… his name's Samuel."

"Who cares, Rick?"

"*You* should—he worked in *your* office—*this* office!" Rick bit back the rest, fighting the almost overwhelming need to punch on this new sheriff's nose and ending up in a cell himself. This wouldn't look good when both of them were up for re-election. For a fleeting second, he wondered who would lock them up.

The sheriff scowled. "Samuel was a full time drunk and a part time FBI agent. He knew the risks. Comes with the territory."

## 4

# CALLING THE SHOTS

Cathy Wilson had been a rural public health nurse for almost twenty years. She had seen a lot of things from visiting trapper hermits, Covid and TB outbreaks, measles, remote home schools, free range kids and attending one bush plane crash. Truthfully the bush plane crash was caused by her husband Dan, who was a crummy pilot. He flew on his own these days. Word gets around.

Each day was a new experience for Cathy.

She glanced into the rear-view mirror as she drove, noticing more gray hair. Almost forty-five years old and she was still marooned in Maclean, Alaska. Damn.

She was now aiming for the commune camp, driving a narrow dirt road with the two local ladies assigned to guide her, May and Irene, silently seated in the back seat along with her scales, laptop and pamphlets. She was never left unsupervised in a camp, which chafed to say the least. Cathy was a pro... she had this!

Driving out to the communities ranked high on her odd meter. Other than initial pleasantries about the weather May and Irene fell silent and their shields went up. So tiresome.

Cathy wasn't in a very good mood. She'd just returned from a public health nurse gathering in Fairbanks. It was normally a fun event. Her peers had some great stories.

The drag on the week was hearing a trusted colleague in the Fairbanks office, an old-time pal, announce she was moving south to Oregon. She'd got the job Cathy was counting on. She and Dan had even found someone to buy their farm and all this was now out the window.

To make it worse her last night in her hotel was mortifying, to say the least. It took her a little while to figure out what was going on next door. There were strange noises going on interminably through the paper-thin walls. She finally figured out the guy was on a phone sex line and was shouting into a speaker phone.

'I'm getting close, babe!'

Closer to what? Oh! Eww!

Neither ear plugs nor the front desk were helpful. It went on for three disgusting and embarrassing hours.

She came to the fields of plenty that surrounded the community. They were bright with large square patches of yellow Canola flowers, meadows scented with clover blossoms, and sections of hay and barley in constant motion, endless lazy waves of green. Idyllic.

It changed as she pulled through the inner gate. Cathy shuddered as she steered into the center of the community. Everyone stopped what they were doing and watched her and her car intently. It was like being in a zombie or western movie.

High noon at Dead Man's Flats.

Everyone was simply but cleanly dressed. The men were in simple shirts and overalls while the women wore dresses or skirts, blouses, and hats. Nineteen sixties.

The buildings were made of crude cut lumber with few windows. The only effort at painting them was a simple preservative of a diesel and oil mix to stop the rot as well as blackening the siding. She could barely smell it, so it was done about five years ago. Lucky nobody in the communities seemed to smoke.

This was one of a number of old army camps, hurriedly built

during the Cold War in the nineteen eighties. Drab and hard to see from the air especially after scrub trees and grass grew in.

There were no flowers or color in the camp except for designated vegetable patches which were huge and lush. Everything growing had to pull its weight.

From the road she noticed the workers had made progress in the fields formerly covered with scrub trees, buck brush and deep grass. Despite using horses, the community dwellers, or citizens as they called themselves, managed to plow all around the camp.

Back breaking and slow but needing nothing from the outside world.

Dan scoffed at their idea of farming with horses. "That's crazy. I could go over there with a cat and a brush plough and clean off everything they're doing, in a week. Then I could get my big Cougar tractor and plow it all afterwards in a couple of days. Done!"

"It's the way they want to do things, Dan. It might even be a condition of getting a homestead. It's a special green thing, I suppose."

"Why do they get such a big spot to do poor farming? I'd doubt they even know what grows here. That's one of those big old military reserve areas the government owns. They can house the troops and have war games out there."

"You have such an imagination."

"It's a good thing those dimwits are giving those blood sucking leaders all their money. Hopefully he'll feed them with it when they can't grow enough food."

Cathy shook her head. "I think they said they had to be entirely self-sufficient according to the terms of homesteading that land."

"Good luck with that. Marcel had a couple of those...citizens... work at the logging camp. Good workers but he said after work those skinny bastards ate free logging camp food until they were sick. You'd think they hadn't eaten in a year."

Cathy shook Dan thoughts from her mind and carefully turned her government SUV around in the parking lot, so she faced out of the entrance.

She announced to her passengers, "We have a rule. We park so we drive straight out. That's the safest so we don't back over kids." *And I can hustle out of this crazy ass place in a hurry, if pressed.*

She carefully aligned her car for a straight out 'Bank robber getaway'.

As an outsider she'd been invited and made a point of calling ahead, but you never knew. There were two dozen of these communities in the state and some nurses weren't welcome.

The leader of this community was letting her in reluctantly, suspiciously and possibly under protest. Were they spies coming for their kids...the tax man...men in black with microchips for them all?

May and Irene got out of the car and headed over to the home that was day care for all their small kids. Cathy scanned the buildings around her noticing a school, barn, sheds and what looked like a wash house for laundry and bathing. She had one more glance at the entrance gate, so she knew the quickest way out.

May and Irene were back. They invited her into the community hall where the vaccinations would take place.

In the community hall Cathy saw a large wooden table which she covered with a clean new piece of plastic then organized her equipment and laid out the pamphlets. She kept her laptop computer near her right arm. The batteries should last for the clinic.

She set up her scales to weigh babies, a bundle of pamphlets about birth control, nutrition, a special birth records chip for her computer, case of vaccines and her nurse's bag. Mothers and children were gathering as she used disinfectant and Cavi-wipes to clean off the tablecloth and her equipment.

The older children looked at her and all her paraphernalia as if she just flew in from Mars. Apparently, a matching powder blue pantsuit is not the usual, out here.

Cathy was kept busy with a constant stream of children and a few young adults getting vaccinated. She was making good progress through the long line of nervous people. Some parents had a list that came from, 'The Lord' for certain shots for some and not for others. She assumed someone in the camp was a self-proclaimed medical expert.

She leaned over a six-year-old, near the end of the line, swabbed a spot on his upper arm and brought out her vaccination needle. "It's all right Hans. Relax."

The little boy squirmed a bit but didn't make a sound. Cathy pulled out the needle and monitored him for signs of a reaction. His face went white as he looked to the doorway. His eyes got big and his mouth fell open.

For a second Cathy thought she might have a medical issue then she turned to where the boy was focused. A big, wide, menacing man with a long staff blocked out the sun in the doorway. He paused, then stepped through. The building went silent.

He strode into the hall towards them while the mothers and children all looked up in fear. One of the women nervously offered, 'Only trust us and our Lord, Brother Isaac."

Cathy kept calm, focused on the man and smiled. "Hello. Are you here for a vaccination?"

The man showed no emotion. "Vaccines are the devil's work."

The room held its breath.

---

IT WAS LATE. Randolph Hobson walked by the security men in the World Oil Corp. building. They never made eye contact.

He got into the elevator, tapped '2' which took him to his temporary cum permanent apartment. Everyone quietly knew it became permanent the day his wife and family left him and moved far away, never to be seen again.

Hiding or dead?

He flipped on the lights as he entered and immediately went to his liquor bar and poured himself a stiff cognac. From the bar he went to his favourite chair, plush with crushed velvet made in Persia in the 1800's. He fell into it carelessly.

Randolph drank in silence until his exquisite crystal goblet was empty. He got up for another and returned to his lonely perch to contemplate his life.

After a big sigh he did what he always did each and every night since she'd left him. He slid open a drawer in his nearby desk and retrieved a worn and haggard letter. This would be the 612th time he'd read it. The words never changed.

*Dear Randolph,*

*I'm sorry to have to leave you this goodbye note but there was no other option. The political murk you and Milton have been immersed in has us fearing for our lives. You won't find me, Fran or Kendra ever again.*

*You were once a good man Randolph. We all loved you. Then you embraced the Disciples.*

*I didn't realize how bad it was until the convention. Setting up a presidential assassination? Planning to put Bill Page in his place? I can hardly believe it of you, still. Thank God you failed. And all those poor people who paid the price along the way.*

*Your wild schemes have made us afraid of you. I've gone to great lengths to ensure you never contact us again. Don't even try. I have enough stored information about you, Milton, and the Disciples to have you both locked up forever.*

*Kay*

Randolph carefully re-folded the letter and put it back in the drawer. He shed a few tears like he always did.

He'd tried finding them but maybe his brother Milton found them first.

---

IN LONDON, Amelia watched as the man with crutches and a beard in front of them say, "Hello. Mr. McBain is sick today and I'll be your instructor until he gets well. I'm Richard Graham."

As the students watched in astonishment, he laid down his crutches, straightened his bent posture and calmly removed his beard, transforming from a bedraggled person to a healthy man of about thirty. He was tall, blue eyed and quite good looking.

"My background is in a little firm you may know...MI5. England is a quieter, gentler place more concerned with losing one's knitting needles and umbrellas these days. Naturally, I was sacked along with hundreds of others. So here I am, a 'spy' one minute, a grocery packer the next, and now a teacher." He gave them all a brilliant smile.

Next, he went through the roll call giving a wink with each name, receiving a grunt from the person in return. After the twenty names were called out, he walked to the front of the class, closed his eyes and rattled off each name in order of seating. Nice party trick, if you were into that sort of thing. A perfect recital.

Except he missed Amelia's name.

---

CORONER RICK FOREST waited until he heard the sheriff leave, get in his car and drive away. This was Tuesday. The sheriff's usual habit was to make his way to a community to mooch a piece of pie and look over the unattached ladies.

He was useless.

Rick pulled his vet bag out from under the bench where Samuel resided, then neatly stacked the tools he would need—saws, scalpels, clippers, bowls, weight scales, bottled water, sutures—on a stretch of clean cloth he'd laid out on a nearby bench. Once he was satisfied he could easily reach everything he needed, he leaned a little camera over his left shoulder to record the autopsy.

Gazing regretfully at Samuel's alabaster body as he pulled on his gloves, he mumbled, "Sorry Sam. We were pals and I hate to do this, but this is our only hope of finding out what happened before the sheriff destroys the evidence in the crematorium. We need to know what the hell they did to you out there—officially and on the record."

Samuel said nothing, of course, something that never happened when the gregarious man had been alive.

Taking another steadying breath, Rick added to no one in particular, "Here lies another soul owed the humble truth of his passing. I've autopsied almost every critter that walks, grunts, milks and flies. A human is the simplest of them all but the only one with a soul…in this case Sam's."

His thoughts swept to the bottle of whiskey he kept in the nearby desk for special occasions but sadly it was empty. With his left hand steadying the corpse, he made the first slice of the "Y' incision across Samuel's chest with his right, methodically cutting and recording as he proceeded.

Rick had autopsied every type of animal over the years. Sometimes he autopsied a bucket of animal guts left in a pail on his doorstep. A farmer found a pig, calf, or horse dead and needed to know what killed it before it spread to the remainder of the herd.

Cutting up Samuel was tidier than a domestic animal, but it still gave him the creeps to have that impassive human face watching and judging him as he sawed and pawed through the chest.

THE PEOPLE in the community hall were stunned silent. The big Angel Enforcer swept his staff across Cathy Wilson's worktable scattering everything all over the place. She did grab vital laptop before it hit the wooden floor. She looked down at the floor to see where her stuff went, horrified and shocked.

The clinic had gone to hell in an instant.

Impressed with his own power, Angel Isaac blissfully glanced down at the floor. He spotted something familiar and leaned over to get it. Bonus! It was a computer chip with an official tag on it. He had no idea what the medical terms printed on it meant but it did look expensive and valuable.

"What is this?" he asked, rage suddenly over.

Cathy nervously managed, "It records the births of babies. If a child is born out here, under a mid-wife's care, its birth stats must be recorded."

"Why?" Isaac demanded, snapping back into predator mode.

"So…so we can track them on the national data base for shots and health history, among other things. Some children have different vaccination schedules. We have to be mindful of—"

"So the government can track us? Tax us? Watch us!"

"No, nothing that ...insidious. Vaccinations must be done in a safe..."

"Are you done here?" Isaac cut her off, taking in the quaking families that stood around them, his gaze glowering person to person. His gaze on made her cringe.

Cathy gasped, "Um...Yes... ah... I was just answering any questions they may have."

"Then leave!"

Everyone in the room was stunned. Cathy was frozen to her chair.

"Leave! Leave *now!*" Isaac slammed his long wooden staff on the table and swept any remaining medical equipment from the table and onto the floor with a noisy clatter. Cathy was lucky to save her weigh scales. Frozen in place, she sat, clutching it to her chest as armor against Isaac's next blow.

Towering over her, he bellowed, "Get the hell outta here!"

He didn't have to say it twice.

---

TERRY AND JESS strode from the cookhouse out into the path between the buildings. When they emerged, Jess led her along the perimeter of the vegetable gardens which were edged with cheerful tall sunflowers staring up to the sky, soaking in every minute of sunlight available.

Two over-sized, clumsy pups challenged and yapped at them but were easily shooed away, their tails still wagging. They seemed to think they were briefly being played with and that made them happy.

Terry and Jess climbed the shallow hill to a freshly ploughed field which was gouged out of the brush and timber at great effort. At the near side of the field, they were met by a tall, thin, older man dressed in worn coveralls. He wordlessly hiked to the waiting pair of young horses attached to a rough wooden sled on skids. Clearly an old pro.

Jess pointed at him. "...this is Gina."

He nodded and barely smiled. Then he gently shook the reins. The horses started their daily shuffle in the dirt. It was obvious he expected the Reids to follow behind on foot. They silently walked and tossed rocks onto the rude wooden sled as the birds sang nearby.

Terry trotted up beside the driver and asked, "Hi... is this called a 'stone boat'?

He grunted and looked at her as if he was just waking up. "I suppose."

"Ah. It's classier than calling it a box of rocks, eh?" Terry grinned at him. He didn't grin in return.

She dropped back to walk alongside Jess. "Where's 'sense of humour' in the bible?"

The driver heard her and replied, "Not sure there is one."

"Exactly."

He managed a sly smile. "But there should be."

They all giggled, then shuffled along, picked up various sized rocks and threw them into the stone boat.

Terry thought to herself, time passes slowly when you're picking up rocks.

At first all the rocks looked the same, some bigger than others, some very small. Terry began to see the difference in color and type of rock.

"Where do these rocks come from Des?"

"A glacier might have dropped them. The ground freezes and eventually squirts the rock to the surface."

"Why are these rocks a problem?"

"Plough and horse ankle breakers."

"Ah."

Des trudged along, guiding and controlling the skittish horses.

Jess took a breath as she heaved a big squarish stone into the back of the boat. *Crunch!* "This field was roughly ploughed, one pass at a time. Each pass hits dozens of rocks of all sizes, migrating to the light like a living thing. Rocks are a constant misery for any field work, spring or fall."

Terry glanced at Des who was fussing over a horse harness and distracted then whispered to Jess, "He doesn't pick rocks with us?"

"Not usually. Women's work. He only lets go of the reins if a very large rock required his assistance. He's here to guide us."

"Guiding seems quite popular around here. Where are we being guided to and for what purpose?"

"That's the big question."

Terry heard the sound of a roaring vehicle engine. She glanced over in time to see a dirty white Alaska Health car speed out of the community like it was being chased by a posse. A shower of gravel and dust followed it down the road. The driver wasn't very steady.

*I'll bet there's a story behind that.*

Their horse driver didn't look up at the sounds of the car as he was preoccupied with a horse's foot. He stopped the beasts and lifted a foot to scrutinize it.

"Hey, I have a horse with a shoe falling off. Go to lunch while I get this fixed."

"Horse blown a tire?" said Terry, expecting some laughs and getting none.

Jess sighed impatiently at Terry's humour attempts. "Come, the lunch wagon arrived early. We get the pick of the lunch bags."

Together they marched along the path leading from the new field to the top of the next knoll where the lunch wagon stood. A little fire was being started to keep the tea warm.

The sun was at the peak of its powers, vanquishing the sparkling dew and warming the land. It was almost eleven thirty and everything under the wide blue sky felt lush and green. Terry and Jess were in the shade of a food wagon skeptically considering what was presented as today's lunch. After exchanging glances to ensure their thoughts weren't overheard, they both sat down.

Jess opened the simple green bag with the sewn-on smile and looked suspiciously through the sad bun-wich. "No critters, fresh, meat isn't green and a bottle of some orange—"

"Kool-aid?" Terry suggested with a wolfish smile. "*You* drink the Kool-Aid first."

Jess sat there blankly, not getting the inside joke.

"Get it? Old cult thing? Didn't go well?

46

"Ah! 'Jones' thing. It wasn't Kool-Aid but something called Flavour Aid. Little known fact."

"Joke, kid?"

"Ha ha. Bringing up the old Jonestown cult isn't a good idea. I've already witnessed more than a few obvious similarities to this place. Let's skip this conversation, shall we?"

Terry shrugged.

"Eat, then pee. We only get a half an hour before a goon comes by with his big wooden staff to remind us how unimportant we really are."

Between bites Terry grumbled, "Picking rocks is such a crappy job. This is backbreaking."

"And make sure we don't make the lunch wagon wait or La Goon comes by and whacks you with his staff."

"I'll bet he doesn't whack me."

Jess glowered at her. "We're here to see if my father's here. Don't get us booted out! Remember our mission."

Terry counted to five and puffed out a breath, pacing herself. She was here to support Jess and had best keep such thoughts to herself. "Sorry kid. Of course. I'll keep my cool so we find dear old dad. Gotcha."

They ate in stony silence, watching the scene around them from their knoll overlooking the area. It was impressive. The community was in the center and surrounded by fields of various crops. Cows, sheep, horses and goats lazily grazed grassy fields.

Jess handed out an olive branch. "See the cattle field and the sheep fields? What do you notice?"

"Ah. The cattle field has more grass and the sheep seem to be in a dirt field?"

"Yup. Sheep will eat the grass right down to dirt while the cattle leave a little to grow later. Gotta rotate them around the fields."

"And you know this because?"

"I was listening while waiting for you. Learning by eavesdropping."

"Clever girl."

"That's me."

"And is that a donkey in with the sheep?" asked Terry who stopped chewing mid mouthful. "...and could this be a donkey bun-wich?"

Jess smiled, "Why not? You must have eaten donkey or worse before in all your travels. You said you ate camel eyes once."

"I said I actually *saw* people eating camel eyes. I didn't eat any." Terry took a breath. "I never ask what type of critter I'm eating while I'm on the job in the nether regions. Besides, I'm not sure donkey meat works for me back in western civilization."

"Relax auntie. The donkeys are like guard dogs for sheep and cows. Coyotes and such predators are terrified of them. They have that weird bray sound then they chase it, bite it behind the neck and shake it. Crabby beasts. Ever watch 'Shrek'?"

"Shrek?"

"Old movie? Green ogre? Never mind. I think we're eating a wild moose, anyways...roadkill."

"Dandy." Terry took a barely comfortable bite.

Jess thought it a good time to change the subject. "Wow, this place looks like a landscape painting. Beautiful. Look at the latest fields. They've been doing the work with horses for weeks."

Terry nodded. "Six 'stone boats' and pickers working them, too.

"Yup, never ending job. Look, one is dumping the rocks near the fence line."

"That's a lot of rocks. And that's quite a rock pile near the entrance way, too."

"I'll say."

"Is that guy building more wall with them? I can't quite make out what he's doing."

"Eyes getting old, Auntie?" said Jess with a mouthful.

"Would seem so. Happens to the best of us."

Jess finished chewing. "Yup. Rocks are a basic building material around here. They use them to build living quarters, kitchens, pantries, classroom school space, storage sheds, workhouses, entrance guard houses."

When Terry didn't respond, Jess waved down the narrow road the Alaska Health car had so recently escaped along. "Walls?"

Terry's eyebrows went up. "Bullet and vehicle proof fortifications. I saw those in Afghanistan. Some have been there for millennia."

"And the Normans in England used them."

"And here we are helping to build walls in Alaska and making history. Walls for Motion." She winked at Jess with a show of sass she didn't 'sell' and took another bite of the sandwich.

## 5

# A SECRET MESSAGE

Amelia found the school day with this new instructor most peculiar. He was smart yet odd. A personality that didn't add up. Pity Terry or Jess weren't around to talk this through with her. They'd know what to do.

She glanced again at her phone wondering how the Reids were doing on their latest adventure. It wasn't their usual mission start, though. So personal.

She re-read Jess's last message, which essentially said, "Looking for my dad in Maclean, Alaska. Tell Terry," and shook her head, still mystified. She'd just have to wait and see how this all panned out.

WITH THE SOUND of Isaac's bellowing in the background, May and Irene urgently helped load Cathy's equipment into her vehicle, the helter-skelter before stepping back and away, their gazes averted from Cathy's.

Isaac came out of the building to tower over the three cowering women and government car, pointing his staff at the gate. Not needing any further encouragement, Cathy scrambled to her car, leaped in and slammed the door. Thankfully it started first try with her key. Gripping the wheel tightly she roared through the gate with a heavy foot and a few cuss words.

She glanced in her rear-view mirror and saw May and Irene standing in the driveway, eating her dust. They looked angry, embarrassed and saddened all at once. Those poor people.

It took Cathy several miles before she was able to unclench her fingers on the wheel. Glancing back at herself in the rear-view mirror, she squeaked, "You're lucky my husband Dan wasn't here, jerk." She was going to phone him then decided against it.

On second thought it was best Dan didn't hear about this. He might blow a fuse, beat Isaac to a pulp and then bulldoze the camp. Bad idea.

Then she remembered the chip the Angel had questioned her about. She stuck out her right hand and tamped around the seat looking for it, her car wobbling drunkenly as she did. "Oh-no! He kept my baby birth-chip! Damn!" The car lurched into the other lane, alarming her. A car accident wouldn't help her day.

No going back for the chip.

When the community finally vanished from her rear-view mirror Cathy guided the car over to the side of the gravel road to pull herself together. She took a deep breath, a swig from her water bottle, then after several minutes of quiet and no sign she was being chased— crazy she would think that, but hey, the guy had been freaking scary— she climbed out the door and peeked at the backseat mess.

Dang!

Before pawing through that rubble she had to make a run to the bush to go pee. As she stepped past the thorn bushes and fallen logs, she watched for passing vehicles that sure as hell would stop and helpfully call out, 'Are ya okay Nurse'? 'Yup!' Or a bus load of tourists ...or a bear might wander by, curious.

Best make it fast.

Her pant suit was something from San Francisco so it required some effort to wriggle out of but she managed. She inevitably managed to get pee on one shoe. Minor detail, today.

Mission accomplished she pulled up her suit and picked her way back to her car while wiping her hands with a cavi-wipe. She dropped her head in annoyance as she opened the rear door. What a mess! By and large, everything appeared to present. She was lucky May and Irene pitched in to help load up or she might not have come away with any of it otherwise.

A few tears spilled out despite her vigilance. She leaned in and scooped the red and blue pamphlets together into a heap and began sorting them, her hands still trembling. Thankfully she'd at least been able to give out a few of these. One pamphlet on birth control was all bent and beat up and unusable. Just as she was about to discard it, she noticed there was hurried handwriting on the back with a crude diagram below the message, *"Another body is buried here. X marks the spot".*

Another body?

---

MAY AND IRENE stood in the dust watching the public health nurse vanish down the road. Cathy wouldn't be back nor would any of her staff.

May shook her head. "Well, there goes another one."

Irene nodded in agreement. "At least we have to go to town for the kids' shots from now on."

May smiled. "Works for me. A few trips to the city"

They quietly had a high five, sure nobody was watching.

---

AMELIA SAT in her school seat lost in her thoughts of what had happened last week. When Terry returned to the London mansion from some crime caper in France, Amelia had told her to see Gulinda, who'd received Jess's message. "I was at school and Jess couldn't wait so she told Gulinda. She'll tell us."

Together they went into Terry's detective office and found

Gulinda sitting blankly at the desk.

"Gulinda! How's it going?"

"Going, Theresa Reid?"

"Yup. How's life and such. Just a saying."

"Ah, a courtesy."

"Gotcha. Your reply could be 'finer than frog's hair' or 'happy as a clam'."

Gulinda seemed puzzled by this, as Terry had intended. "Can a clam's positive emotional state be measured? I was unaware frogs had hair, Ms. Reid."

"Amelia will explain it all to you, Gulinda," assured Terry with a huge smile.

Amelia looked exasperated at Terry's request but moved on. "Gulinda; Go ahead and play Jess's message to Terry."

Gulinda smiled, seemed to exercise her voice. She then spoke in a perfect Jess voice complete with pauses and inflections. She was scary accurate.

*"Aunty Terry,*

*I received an old letter about the real father I never knew. He's off the grid in some cult community that's "Back to nature" up in MacLean, Alaska.*

*I made a decision to boldly go and try to find him,*

*Love, Jess*

*PS you are welcome to join me.*

Amelia was impressed at how Gulinda mimicked Jess's voice to perfection.

"Did Jess say where MacLean, Alaska is?"

"No."

"Directions?"

"Zero."

They stood in silence as Terry thought. Gulinda might be pondering frogs and clams.

Terry broke the spell. "Amelia. Guard the Phillimore!"

"Me? By myself?"

"Yes. Ask Gulinda if you have any questions."

"Gulinda, this robot-something?" Amelia thought Gulinda looked hurt by her remark but wasn't sure. How could she tell?

"You'll have so much to talk about in any voice you want. Order pizza with Winston Churchill's voice. The fun you'll have. Work it out until we return."

"And that will be...?"

"Um... sometime-ish. No internet there except my KGB bat phone. Gotta find a lost dad."

"But..."

"Be cool and stay in school. Bye!"

The front door slammed, and Amelia was all alone.

Terry's mechanical General Unsupervised Learning—GUL—assistant stood, looking her way with unfocused eyes. "Amelia; Are you finer than frog's hair?"

"Fine, I think."

"It is a mid-nineteenth century American simile," Gulinda recited.

"No doubt." *And here I am, talking to inanimate objects.*

---

Nurse Cathy Wilson was furious as she drove into the Health Center of Maclean, Alaska's parking lot. She gathered her reports from her car, kicked the door closed with her foot and stomped into the office of her area Medical Health Officer.

Dr. Wendy Forest looked up from her desk. "Hi Cathy. How did the community visit go...?"

Cathy dropped her document bag on the floor and flopped down in a chair opposite, her legs splayed. "God, it was horrible! One of their goons ran me off and stole my chip for live births. They're getting worse out there. Beverly Hillbillies meets Hogan's Heroes!"

"Take a breath Cathy. Here, have this cup of tea—no germs yet, I promise. It looks like you need it more than me. Let's go through this step-by-step."

Cathy needed both hands to steady the *Best Nurse in the World* teacup for a good drink. "I had a request by the East Community for a vaccination series. I got there, backed in, thankfully, set up, gave out thirty-six shots and boosters. An Angel Enforcer asshat marched in and started shouting at me to leave. I scooped up my stuff and drove away. It looks like he grabbed the birth-chip in the confusion."

Dr. Forest looked at her, concerned. "Another birth-chip?"

"Yes. I'll bet they use it to hack in and scam baby bonus money for nonexistent children. It may be the only reason they let me in there."

Dr. Forest shook her head. "Dang."

"That's not the worst of it." Cathy passed a piece of paper to the doctor before pushing the door closed.

*'Another body is buried here. X marks the spot.'*

"Geez!"

Cathy looked closely at the doctor. "Another one! Did anything happen with the last message?"

"I passed it on to the new Sheriff. I pestered him for weeks and all he would say was it was a prank and forget about it."

---

ISAAC WAS PLEASED to have cleared off the nosy nurse. There were always grumblings among the people after she left, sowing discontent. Brother Lionel should never have let her in. Let the disgruntled families leave. Where would they go? The community had their money and property. Let them hitchhike with the clothes on their backs.

Any people that leave will be stranded for life in the hole of a town, MacLean, and be forced to send part of any money they make back to the commune owners, anyway. They should have read the agreement they signed when they joined.

He pointed at May and Irene. "Come here."

Terrified, they came closer, but not within staff whacking distance.

He raised himself up, towering over them. "Did you tell anyone about Brother Samuel being buried?"

Frightened, they both shook their heads.

"Are you sure? The cops came and dug him up Monday night. Someone had to tell about it. Was it any of you?"

The group crowded together like frightened baby ducks. The hall was deathly quiet except for a little boy who started crying.

Jeb looked at everyone, face by face, hard and grim. "Nobody goes to town until I find out who squealed! Get back to your duties before I really blow my top!"

They scattered like frightened mice.

---

AFTER A SIXTEEN-HOUR WORKDAY picking rocks Terry and Jess ate a feeble supper of greasy meatloaf, boiled potatoes and some wild boiled tea.

"No ketchup? I can't eat meatloaf without ketchup," Terry grumbled.

Jess ignored her, plowing her tin fork through the mystery-meat meatloaf.

Terry added, "Where are the showers?"

"Showers happen only once every four days."

"I'm doing it on my own time."

"Doesn't matter. Water and soap are precious."

"And they control it?"

"They control everything. I thought you army types could handle this?"

"I can…when I'm not paying for it."

"And paid for it with a phony person's money…*Gina*."

"Touché!" Terry smiled. "It's the principle of the thing, kid."

A voice disturbed her day-dream musings.

---

ISAAC STRODE into Lionel's office, sporting a giant smile. "I have another baby birth-chip for you!"

Lionel stopped what he was doing. "Today's nurse?"

"Yes. Hack it and it's yours. We need those nurses to visit more often."

"Excellent." Lionel plugged in the chip, hacked the login and scanned the listing. Murmuring under his breath with satisfaction, "Another thirty-two births we can register. Another thirty-two child benefits bonuses from the government."

"You look up the obituaries for birthdays of newborns deceased at birth?"

"Who told you that?"

"Just a guess. Makes sense." Isaac grinned. "Half a million for us all?"

Lionel looked at him with narrowed eyes. "Us? This money will do the Lords work. You may go."

Isaac left annoyed. And how much of this goes into Lionel's pockets?

———

"YOU ARE special and here to serve the Lords purpose," Lionel Garson called out as he marched into the cookhouse. He stopped, impatiently waiting for the citizens to eat their meagre evening meal. When he decided they were done he strutted up to the lectern in the corner and set down his bible and notes. He spread his arms in a quiet command for silence and the people hushed with Jeb and Isaac watching closely from the wings, staffs at the ready.

"Some women choose minor roles in serving the church while gaining their greatest joy and sense of accomplishment from being wives and mothers, some abandon these ordained roles creating chaos and confusion regarding the role of women both in ministry and in the home. Women must follow scripture in order to know that role.

"Women must know their place is to do as men direct them as we all do God's work.

"Remember: you are special and here to serve the Lord's purpose.

"Let us pray."

———

AFTER THE EVENING PEP TALK, Terry and Jess made their way back to the bunkhouse in darkness. Terry said, "I'm fried. This rock picking is a good workout."

"The days are long."

"You've been at this for a month, Jess?"

"Time flies when you're picking rocks."

"Evening entertainment, kid?"

"Nope. Work late, then the religious pep talk, then bed-time."

"No holy choirs, guitar sing-alongs around the campfire and roasting marshmallows? Where are the cowboy hats? They showed all that on their brochure."

"Daily toil on the work gang, then bed."

"I'm complaining to my travel agent."

Once in their room Terry had a quick look around and under their beds.

"Looking for something, Auntie?"

Terry winked, "You never know."

After a bird bath from cold water in a steel basin they were both in bed.

Terry lay awake for a while wondering how they'd ended up in this strange place. She'd been surprised at how easy it was to come to Maclean and get a ride to the camp. The paperwork was simple for her to fudge. It was clear the communities wanted warm bodies first and foremost. Once the people were on site, they were policed by the Angels. After what she'd witnessed last night, she now believed if the Angels sussed out an informer, that informer would likely end up buried in the middle of a field.

She'd best avoid that part.

---

CORONER RICK FOREST wearily came home, scraping off his shoes in the entranceway. He headed to the shower and put on jeans and a T-shirt Wendy had given him for his birthday, *'Don't Argue with a Veterinarian – They Neuter!'*

Something smelled good.

"Supper in ten minutes, Rick!"

He was pleased with Wendy, his wife of four years, or 'Number Five' as his son Jack called her. His son quickly became estranged as the number of wives Rick acquired accelerated. He should just phone Jack and say hi and break the ice…someday.

He wasn't sure if Jack was kidding about distancing himself from his father or was seriously disgusted at all the wives Rick found over the years. The split from his son saddened him but not enough to change his womanizing ways.

"No more philandering Mr. Rick Forest," was the order from Wife Number Five, Medical Doctor Wendy, the day of their wedding. She followed this by casually mentioning with a smile she could snuff him out and nobody would ever know.

He almost said he could do this too but kept his big mouth shut. She had a funny look in here eye. Shouldn't tempt fate.

A weird marital standoff.

Rick had to admit his various wives had histories.

Sue, wife number one thought he smelled funny. He had to admit he worked on everything from parakeets to ponies to raging bulls and yes, they didn't bathe much. So, in the end, Sue had been correct.

Wife number two, Mavis, decided Rick was having conversations with his animals like Dr. Doolittle. Nope, he just did that to soothe them. "Easy fella…it's okay." No reply. No two-way conversing was happening. So, Mavis had not been correct. Sorry, Mavis, no gold star for you unless you are trying to get me committed.

Number Three, Candy, was the best looking of the lot, built like a beauty queen. She'd run off with a friend—an ex-friend, now—Frank. He'd always hoped to neuter Frank if the opportunity presented itself. Being an optimist, he still lived in hope.

Wife Number Four, Gwen, obligingly jumped off a cliff into the swirling, boiling river and was never found. That one always made him smile—and heave a sigh of relief. Gwen was loopy. Good thing she'd only taken herself out. Some days, the way she watched him made him believe she had ideas. The sheriff at that time wondered why Gwen didn't leave a suicide note. Wasn't that peculiar?

And here he was with Number Five, Doctor Wendy.

He sat down at the table, wondering what she'd cooked today. She was always experimenting with some new cuisine. They generally were good but there had been a few failures, some heartburn and one fierce case of the trots. Nothing fatal.

Wendy was a doctor, too, but an actual medical physician so Rick assumed she could (would?) resuscitate him if her cooking killed him. Again, he was ever the optimist.

Wendy clunked a plate loaded with food before him. "Try this Rick. It's Ethiopian with a Thai dessert after."

"...um...sure." Rick dug into the steaming, smelly portions. Hot... nice texture...just the right amount of ginger and peppers...the fresh veggies were barely crunchy...not too rich. "It tastes better than it looks."

"Thanks for the compliment...sort of?"

"Sorry. It's good."

They ate in silence.

"How was a day in the life of a crusading veterinarian?" she finally asked, hopefully.

"Calving, today."

"Udder nonsense?" she teased.

Rick kept on eating, oblivious.

"You seem distracted, dear."

"My apologies. I did the autopsy on Samuel today."

"Wow. How did your new sheriff take it?"

"Wasn't interested. I had to perform it while he was at the communities for the day. Not sure what he does up there but it's a huge priority. I think it was for giggles and pie. He wanted me to bury Samuel ASAP."

"What did you find in your autopsy?"

"He had bruises consistent with a beating while seated in a chair. They were all face and frontal. No defensive wounds. Chafing around his wrist and neck."

"Tied in a chair?"

"That's what I was thinking." Rick took another mouthful, grateful Wendy and he could speak of medical subjects that normally put people off. "Sam was tough, so he had to have been restrained. Probably grabbed him when he was drunk."

"What killed him?"

"Petechial hemorrhaging indicated asphyxiation. From the body damage, he didn't go quietly."

"Wow. Just like the others when they're..." She faded off and sipped at her cold beer.

"...in an exorcism?" he offered.

"Or *covered up* by an *apparent* exorcism. Either way, it's bad. What are you going to do about this? From the outside, this looks like an interrogation, a murder and a cover up."

"I recorded the autopsy on my phone and that's where it'll stay for now. Not sure who I can trust."

"There's more you should know." She handed him the note. "I got another message with a crude map, today."

Rick read the note in silence. *Another body is buried here. X marks the spot.*

He grumped, "Not much point in giving this to the sheriff. He did squat last time. I won't waste my time digging this one up."

They ate in silence for some minutes. Wendy's phone beeped and she glanced at the message. "Reminder—don't forget you're playing at Robbie Burns Night, Saturday."

Rick lowered his head. "Geez, how did I get roped into that?"

Wendy laughed, spilling a bit of food from the corner of her mouth. "That's your fault! You hammed it up with your accordion and showed them 'Amazing Grace.'"

He shook his head. "An accordion marching in the Haggis at Robbie Burns night? Could it get worse? Mr. Burns would roll over in his grave."

"Want to borrow my plaid dress for a kilt? Underwear optional," she suggested with a giggle.

"No!"

"I'm coming along to take pictures. You could try the 'kilt' on tonight if you want." She ended the conversation with a suggestive wink and a hearty laugh.

Rick burst into laughter, too. He was tickled by her laugh and her sense of humour. Heartburn or not, she'd stay for a while.

# 6

# FAMILIAR MEETING

Jess went to her dream world, unbidden. She was in the rainy Vancouver alley, hovering over her dead mom. Too familiar.

It was almost cliche.

An apparition of her long-deceased mother, Gloria, appeared, "Hello Jessica M. We haven't spoken for months."

"No. I suppose it's because my life is uneventful."

"Yet, here you are. No more school?"

"Summer break and I'm done high school."

"And my sister Terry?"

"She's been out on various cases for her rich clientele."

"But here you both are in the wilderness. Are you searching for something?"

"Miles Vickers, my father."

Gloria's ghost froze at the name. "That's a name I haven't heard for a long time. Do you think he's here?"

"He might be. Is he my father?"

"Yes. I was in the states for a few months and met him. We had a fling. Turns out he was married. I got the boot from the US and never saw him again."

"I never knew that."

"What can I say? He never showed any interest, so he was forgotten."

"A good man?"

"I think so. He was torn between leaving his wife at a difficult time and running off with me. Between a rock and a hard place, as they say."

"Is he here?"

Gloria shook her head. "It's not my place to say. It's hardly a life-or-death matter in this world I'm in. Doesn't even rate as 'Housekeeping', apparently."

"According to who?"

"You don't want to know."

Jess awoke crying.

Terry was up and at her bedside. "What's up?"

"Same old dream. I'll tell you tomorrow."

"Picking rocks seems to be the best gossip time."

The sun was soon peeking through their window, bringing morning all too soon. They were up and out to the outhouse, breakfast, outhouse again, then off picking rocks.

---

JEB, one of the Angel Enforcers stepped over the lumpy field furrows towards the stone boat, looking at its driver. Doing work by hand with horses was brutal and deathly slow. This guy was no farmer—anyone could see that. But "It was Gods Way". They didn't use any mechanization.

The driver...what's his name... Des. His name was Des, and he was behind schedule in clearing this field. They managed to plough it with the new bigger horses and the ancient 1925 International Genius plow. *Genius*, he scoffed. How ironic. A horse plow in a modern world?

Lionel had directed him to light a fire under Des and the two new girls. According to Lionel's computer projections this field was falling behind. It didn't help when Jeb suggested it was because the team was new.

Picking rocks is the best place to start new help and new horses. Breaks everybody into the routine. Shows the new ones that resistance is futile.

Jeb strode towards Des and the pickers. Des looked right at him, so Jeb waved and told him to stop. He turned away and flicked the reins of the horses.

Jeb was getting the brush off!

Annoyed, he increased his pace, on a mission. He'd pushed around tougher people than an old man and two women.

---

AMELIA SLID out of her warm bed and got ready for her second school day with the substitute instructor, Richard Graham. It had been an odd start, but he seemed to know his cloak and dagger.

She poached two eggs and fried a nice, fat kipper. She smiled to herself at how appalled Jess would have been over a breakfast like this. Jess is probably eating steak and eggs followed by strong coffee hand made by handsome cowboys in ten-gallon hats, whatever that meant.

She called out, "Triplex: News."

*"This is Brock Beckster of the BBC reporting on the body found in the Pickadilly east entrance of the tube, yesterday morning. The police aren't releasing details pending positive identification. He has been described as a man in his sixties. Foul play is suspected."*

That's not far from where I get on the tube.

She dashed around and headed for the subway and the quick trip to school. This time she built in more time to see if she was followed.

The subway station buzzed with activity. People were rushing in all directions grateful the system was working. The usual sad buskers stood in little nooks and crannies, thrilled they could make a bit of cash today. None looked like Gomez and Karl.

She boldly marched into the tube train deliberately going in the wrong direction, standing until the doors almost closed on her, bursting out in the nick of time. Glancing down she made sure her bag wasn't grabbed by the doors. She went up one level and caught the next train going to school, went one block and got out.

Pausing in the doorway to the washrooms she watched to see who hurried to keep up. There was an old man looking suspicious, but she could see he was just old. Nobody followed. She needed to get to school.

"Good morning, Amelia Pun."

She jumped at hearing the voice and turned to the source. It was the new school instructor, Richard Graham.

"Sorry to scare you. I live around here. Are you coming to school?"

She felt stupid. He couldn't have been following her. "Yes, I'm going to school, Mr. Graham."

"Call me Richard. Shall we go?"

Feeling foolish she followed along. Very nice looking fellow. They sat together in the train, in an awkward silence.

"I'm sorry I missed your name, yesterday. I was trying so hard to make a good impression."

She nodded. "It's all good."

They sat watching a homeless elderly lady in shabby black clothing open her umbrella, forcing people nearby to move over.

"This is an off the wall question, but a girl also named Amelia Pun went around the moon in the Quantum spaceship last year. Wouldn't that be an amazing trip?"

Amelia didn't want to brag or boast but she thought Mr. MI5 might be impressed. "That was me. I got a trip on the Quantum."

"You are the space traveller in my class? That's incredible."

"It was. Gives me goose bumps thinking about it."

---

TERRY SPOTTED one of the enforcers headed their way. Maybe he found the worm in his bun yesterday and this was payback? She watched him approach from the corner of her eye but kept on picking.

She and Jess walked close to the horses and driver and continued picking various sized stones and flinging them into the sled. Being closer was easier on the arm. Having Jeb, the enforcer, heading their way sped up the stone boat and rock picking. Des must know a visit from Jeb was not a good thing.

Terry made a point of staying near Des to hear what was going on. Jeb tripped awkwardly along the rough ground. He chose a wider furrow which allowed him to intercept them sooner.

Seeing this, Jess snuck away to the other side of the horses. Maybe she thought she could avoid the upcoming one-sided battle?

"Stop!" Jeb shouted, gasping for air.

Des pulled back on the reins and looked at him nervously. "Only trust us and our Lord."

Jeb gasped harshly between breaths, "Why are you working so slowly? We need this area ready to plant but it's still full of rocks!"

"The Lord left us more rocks with which to build more homes and protect our flocks. A blessing," said Des.

"Shut your yap. We need this area done in the next couple of days. No lunch or supper break today. Work until the sun is down."

Des protested, "That's almost midnight!"

Terry moved closer, nearer the men, enjoying the distraction of a field spat. "Oh, there's a nice little rock right there." She lifted it and came closer, chucking it into the back. The men ignored her.

The sled driver looked over the horses and the workers. "That is more than man or beast can take. Plus, we'll miss Prophet Garson's evening prayers which I dearly look forward to."

"These horses and women are meant to work the fields."

Terry didn't like the sound of that.

"We are all working for the Lord," Des insisted.

"Are you arguing with me?" Jeb showed a rumble of temper, lashing out with his long staff which he'd aimed at Des's face.

Terry's hand flashed out, catching the staff midair. She looked at Angel Jeb, smiling, pointing her finger at him, "Come on buddy. You're wasting valuable rock picking time. Let's all just get back to work. The Lord won't make those rocks jump in there all by themselves."

He glowered at her. "This is none of your concern, woman."

"I gave you that tasty bun, remember? Another one tomorrow if you play your cards right." *Only if it has worms.*

He jerked his staff free and marched away in angry, uneven stumbles across the furrows. It was difficult to appear powerful when you ran like a rat, Terry thought charitably.

Des watched Jeb leave, seeming both frightened and relieved. "Thank you for saving me a beating. Bless his heart but he gets going with his staff in the Lord's name and doesn't stop. He only does what's best for us."

Terry nodded, "I'm sure he's a lovely man, deep down." *Not likely.*

Des stood blankly in awkward silence. "Sorry, I wasn't paying attention before. You are...?"

"Hey, I'm...er...Gina...and Jess is over there waiting for us."

The man stuck out a big worn hand to shake, "Great to formally meet and thank you, Gina. Do call me Des."

"Good to make it official, Des. Shall we get back to work before Mr. Angel with the staff comes back for another whack? Jess has a head start."

---

JESS CRINGED at this upcoming confrontation between her auntie and the angel enforcer. It wouldn't end well especially in her search for her father. She hurried to get ahead of the horse and sled but stayed close enough to hear what was happening.

So much for their cover.

The enforcer's voice was initially solid and stern, getting louder and angry at the end. Her curiosity got the better of her and she glanced over in time to see the guard swinging his staff towards Des.

Terry caught it out of the air!

Her head dropped. Typical. The enforcer was going to get beaten to a pulp and they'd be on the run in the middle of nowhere. No Dad. All this time of snooping and picking rocks for nothing. Dang.

To her surprise it looked like Terry was smiling and being quite diplomatic and the angel didn't have a scratch on him. Who knew auntie could be so smooth?

After a minute the enforcer walked away in a huff, Terry shook hands with the grateful driver, and they went back to work.

No muss, no fuss. They got working again without a word. At eleven thirty she saw the noon lunch wagon arrive and started a fire on the next little hill.

The driver told them, "Let's keep this break as short as possible. Looks like they want us to speed things up. Skip any rocks walnut sized or smaller. Early but short lunch. I'm getting these horses to some water. See you in twenty minutes."

Terry led Jess off to a secluded and shady spot under a tree.

"Was the driver happy you saved him a beating?"

"He was! Shook my hand and said call me 'Des'."

"Des? That's it? I knew that, already."

"I have my suspicions most folks are up her for a reason so nick names or no names are the norm."

"Like 'Gina'?"

"Exactly."

"Hoping he was your dad?"

"Always. I'm not sure what I'd do if I met him. Run up for a hug?"

"Like me when we first met, way-back-when?" Terry teased. "It took a month before you accepted I was your auntie."

"I was a confused semi-homeless kid."

"It's okay Jess. Just teasing. I'm a bit jealous, actually."

"It's all good. What do you suggest we do out here while picking rocks in the wilderness?"

"Let's keep listening and snooping."

"I was going to bawl you out for stopping the enforcer from beating Des, but you made him an ally, hopefully."

"Yes, but we'll have to watch out for Jeb the Enforcer. I'm sure he's asking questions about us now."

# 7

# TOUCHED BY AN ANGEL

Jeb met Isaac and the other "Guiding Angels" at the community hall. Real hot coffee, lasagna and fresh apple pie. He hated eating mush with the crews.

After loading up his tray he sat down beside Isaac and shoveled in the food eagerly. The other enforcers were chowing down as well. A sullen camp citizen came by to take the empty trays with another following to top their coffee cups. They thought they had the best jobs in the camp because they got real coffee and the leftovers.

The new ass-kissing sheriff was here, mooching pie and flirting with the ladies cleaning the tables. Lionel had been slowly bringing him into the community way of doing things. Friends in high places.

Jeb looked around to check he wasn't being heard and said in a low voice, "Any of you met the new recruit, Gina? Mid-thirties, chatty? Isaac and I did yesterday. I was going to whack one of those dim wits and she caught my staff out of the air like it was nothing."

Jeb looked over at the head enforcer, Walt Driscoll, the grim senior man at their table. They all stopped speaking when Walt spoke. "These folks come here with skills and attitudes from all over. She could have a martial arts background. We've had a few over the years but deep down they're sheep."

"Yessir."

Walt put his fork down and looked over his men. "Reminds me. What do we know about the body they dug up Monday night in the west sheep field?"

Isaac nervously said, "It was the old shepherd, Samuel. Died of something so we buried him in that field."

"So, Isaac; how was it authorities found out and dug him up?"

Isaac broke into a sweat at being singled out. "I dunno."

"How many phones do we have out here?"

"Uh, none."

"And how many people are allowed to come and go from this camp?"

"A few, escorted. Once a week."

"Don't you think you could look up who came and went to find out who squealed…you idiots?" Walt scowled.

The table of men nodded and agreed.

"Then get out there and find who squealed! Or would you rather spend a few weeks picking rocks?"

The table cleared as the enforcers scattered.

———

IN LONDON AMELIA scrambled around getting ready for school. Richard Graham was working out very well as a replacement for old Mr. McBain. She enjoyed the fact he didn't give them nearly as much homework.

"Triplex: News."

*"This is Brock Beckster of the BBC reporting on the body found at the Piccadilly east entrance of the tube. The Met Police identified the victim as a Mister Ed McBain, well known criminology instructor. MET Police placed a ban on further details but let slip that it was indeed a murder."*

Mr. McBain? Oh my god!

———

TERRY AND JESS reluctantly climbed out of their warm beds and stood on the cold bunkhouse floor trying not to get a splinter in their toes. The cold water in the wash basin was the first hurdle of the day.

Terry splashed and scrubbed her hands while cheerfully humming a tune. "Happy Birthday to me, happy birthday to me..."

Jess listened in wonder, then asked, "Auntie, is that the birthday song?"

Terry looked over her towel as she dried her face, "Yup."

"This isn't your birthday, is it?"

"Nope. I got used to singing it at cop training school."

"Why?" asked Jess.

"If you wash your hands and sing 'happy birthday' it's the perfect length of time for a proper hand scrub."

Jess looked at her, mystified.

Terry elaborated, "Long story. When I was just a bit older than you, I was in cop school. A pandemic virus panic came to the world and most of the students at our training hall went home but a few of us had nowhere to go and stayed at the hall."

"...and?"

"We couldn't go out and we were bored. Every morning we washed our hands to the birthday song just like the base nurse told us. We modified it a bit with swear words. Want to hear that one?"

"No. What virus?"

"A COVID something virus. It initially scared the shit out of everyone so all had to stay six feet away from other people for quite a while. A couple million died and then a baby boom happened ten months later. Ten million babies!"

"Ah..."

Terry looked at Jess seriously. "It was terrible. A cruise ship came into New York harbour and crashed into the Statue of Liberty. All the people on the ship were killed by the virus. The dying captain was chained to the wheel, steering the ship. That virus spread to the world."

Jess looked at Terry, horrified.

"No way!"

Terry winked, "No foolin'!"

"You're teasing me!"

"Sorry...the virus was true, but the ship was a stretch."

"Really? No kidding!"

"All before your time. They found a vaccine for it, made a zillion bucks and it occasionally comes up on Jeopardy, like Swine Flu."

"I see. Enough tales, Auntie. Time to hear more tales in the square."

"Yes, lead on Jess."

---

LIONEL GARSON LOOKED over his legion shivering in the cold morning mist. They looked to him for a reason for endless back breaking work and these lean times. Lionel found it challenging to make an effective, short sermon for the mornings. Time was money but his message had to be clear for their grand purpose.

He stepped up to the ancient rusty microphone set up on the rickety wooden dais and looked over the crowd.

"The Devil gave thee a nip on the back of thy right hand, for a mark that thou waste one of his number.'"

Lionel paused for effect.

"Beware the 'mark of the devil' which is the way powerful and evil banks control people, hide your life savings, and you can only retrieve it with a hidden code. That magic number will be stamped on the back of your hand with invisible ink."

He was pleased to see most of the crowd examining their hands over for evidence they'd been stamped.

"Do you have that number? I can tell you it's not needed, friends. We've managed, through great effort, to recoup all our savings and you will never need the 'devil' to find it!

A few in the captive crowd cheered weakly.

"Your efforts will be rewarded at the end of days when we will rule over the non-believers and then take our place in the kingdom of heaven. Believe only in us.

"Beware of the 'mark of the devil' from government, banks and other secret societies controlling the money for our just cause with magic numbers and secret passwords.

"As you leave for nourishment be sure and thank angels Walt, Isaac and Jebediah for their protection.

"I shall..." whispered Terry.

"Shhh."

"Remember—you are special and here to serve the Lords purpose, especially those of you serving in the National Guard units.

"Bow your heads in prayer..."

---

TERRY'S EYES popped open with the words "National Guard units" and gasped, glancing over at Jess. She mouthed the words, "Holy crap – National Guard?"

---

DES COULD BARELY DRAG himself into his bed after the long hard day. In the morning, he was up two hours before the pickers, readying the horses for the long workday. At night, while the pickers ate supper and heard the last sermon, he spent two more hours stabling the horses, removing harnesses, rubbing them down, tending to their feet, watering and feeding them.

Just like him, horses were anonymous labour.

Most of the time he was too late for dinner and very little was left. The cooks usually made an effort but there wasn't much to offer.

Sleep was his only reward until the usual dream invaded his thoughts. His restless mind would stir from its dead slumber. Thoughts swirled.

Usual sad dream. He was in his familiar place, standing, looking down on her. His dear wife lay in her hospital bed, gray and weak. Everything in the room was gray, even the flowers in a nearby vase. She was a barely animated corpse. The conversation was always the same.

Drama.

"What are you doing in this camp, Miles? This is a terrible place," the corpse said.

"I'm called 'Des' up here, Melanie."

"Des?"

"Yes, Des. I'm hiding… embarrassed at how my life ended up. I was a drunk living in a car. I don't want anyone finding out. I expect most folks up here are doing the same."

"This community is like the Foreign Legion of farming? Pretend and forget?"

"I did get a guard uniform so we could march around in our off hours."

"They even made you join the National Guard so you have no free time at all!"

"We've been through this. I needed a change. My life was going nowhere."

"Living as a labourer in Alaska doesn't sound like an improvement. Retire somewhere like Tucson or Florida. We have the money." Her voice trailed off from the effort of speaking.

His gentle reply was always the same. "We *don't* have the money, Melanie. You got cancer and we spent every dime keeping you alive? I would do it again."

"The life insurance?"

"No insurance if it's an assisted death, especially when… *I* did it."

"Why did you choose to go to that …commune?"

"Escape. No more medical bills. Mr. 'Miles Vickers' vanishes. Here I'm simply known as Des. They promised we'd be back to the land, working for the lord in his beautiful natural paradise. By and large we are."

"You're a free labourer subsisting under a tight watch. Don't forget that… Des."

"I never do."

Melanie and the bed became blurry and disappeared from his mind. He opened his eyes and shook his head trying to forget. The same dream every night for two and a half years.

Another reminder dream burned into his soul.

---

NEXT MORNING MAY and Irene scrubbed heaps of worn and thread bare shirts, socks with holes, ripped jeans and mud-caked coveralls. Sweat poured down their faces as they filled up the hampers with sodden clothing. Other sweating women took them out and hung them on long clotheslines, pinching them in place with wooden pegs. The clothesline drooped under the weight, straining to keep the garments off the dirt. Sometimes the worn clothesline broke, especially when it was windy. Hopefully not today.

May glanced around and saw they were alone. "Psst...Irene!"

Irene checked for listeners before replying. "Yes?"

"At least this time the kids got their shots before Brother Isaac chased her off."

May had a guarded smile. "True. I forgot you were here for the last nurse visit."

"Yes, when Citizen Gleadow started yelling, 'The vaccines are planting robot chips in the children.'"

"That nurse ran for her life, too."

"Looks like we'll have to go to town if the kids need shots. Not a bad thing. I'll have a look at the little record sheet and find out what they need."

---

TERRY AND JESS sat at the end of the big table to finish off a meagre evening dinner.

"Beans and buns. Mmm," said Terry. "An MRE Army TV dinner would be better, sadly."

"But no worms in the buns. Maybe it would be better *with* them."

"Sorry kid. Gotta draw the line somewhere."

"Shhhh..."

Jeb walked by them, making a point of glancing at his watch. "Ten minutes then back to work."

Jess looked away and kept eating until he was out of ear shot. "I've done worse... and better."

They walked together back to the stone boat in the field. It was a pleasant day with wildflowers mixed in with the long grass along the path.

Des was coming their way with the horses. One was old and gray and the skittish young one was brown. He made sure they were fed and watered, essential on such long days.

"Can I help you hook up the horses, Des?" asked Terry. "I'm always looking for a new skill."

"Sure. Take these reigns. Stand here and back them up to the hitch. Be gentle."

Terry took the reins. "What happens if you aren't gentle?"

"They'll trample you and drag you around the field."

"Good to know."

Terry stood at the back of the horses tugging the reins calling. "Umm...back up?"

To her surprise the horses backed up to the hitch. She reached down, lined it up and dropped in the pin. "Is that it?"

Des grinned. "'Back up' is the magic word. Most people just yank on the reins and shout 'move' or something. Horses know a few word commands."

"I got lucky."

"Why don't you steer them, and I can work the rock pile, too."

"Deal. Why an old horse and a young horse together on a stone boat?"

"The old horse teaches the young horse what to do and the heavy stone boat keeps a skittish horse from galloping around."

"Ah."

"Like you and me... Gina," added Jess with a smirk.

"Get to work, kid!"

Jess watched Terry steering the horses with amazement. "Well done... Gina."

After another exhausting day's work, Terry and Jess went into their little home.

"Do we get the weekend off?"

"Nope. We work on Saturday and Sunday with a one-hour break for church then we're back at it."

"Lords day of rest and all that?"

"Not so much."

"We got showers today! I can pull the sheets over my face and not gag. I feel special."

Jess crawled into her bed and closed her eyes. She had no trouble sleeping around this place. She was dead to the world.

A gentle hand covered her mouth and Terry's face was close to hers. "I'm going for a walk."

She saw Terry in dark clothing and a flashlight headed for the door. There was probably a knife and a gun on her somewhere, too. Her watch said it was two a.m. "What in the world are you up to? On second thought, I don't want to know. Find Dad, remember?"

Terry nodded then silently slipped out the door on some mission. She knew what she was doing.

Jess shook her head and tried to recover her slumber despite a mind active with questions. Her Aunt Terry would get to the bottom of why these communities existed. *Someone* bankrolled these places and went to great effort to see them controlled in a certain way.

"In Motion" had a strange spiritual pull on its inhabitants. So many odd folks, some very talented, some rich, some poor, brought in from all over the world for something called "Only trust us and our Lord".

Jess tossed and turned. She had to admit this simple life did have its attraction. The ceaseless drone of twenty-four-hour reality news barrage had worn her down with endless blather, repetition and advertising. Being in the community meant the unending video game was over and she was enjoying the silence.

Only one source told her what to think as compared to a thousand out in the real world. *Simple is fine for me.*

# 8

## SKULKING AROUND BY MOONLIGHT

Once out the door Terry paused in the dark, listening and surveying the area. The moon had yet to peer over the trees so shadows were plush and would envelop her. The silence was deafening. From the doorway there wasn't a spoken word or a barking dog. Exhausted folks were all in bed, snoring.

Nighttime was best for checking this place out. There would be too many questions asked in daylight. Besides, she had rocks to collect during the day.

She stealthily sneaked along the sides of buildings smothered in the shadows and watched for people coming and going. There were bound to be a few people seeking an outhouse or someone else's mate. First place she checked was the vehicle park. One side had very nice BMW's and deluxe pick-ups for important people. The other end had a few larger, worn farm trucks with wooden boxes on the back.

South of the vehicle park there was a large plot unused by anyone in the camp. She saw the hole where the cops had dug up someone while she and Jess watched. The line of broken shadows of sunken earthen holes indicated quite a few more plots. There were no markers. Forbidden earth.

Serial killer's unmarked graveyard?

She went outside the perimeter of the little homes and went along the ditch, looking and listening. Dogs? Wire? Hidden sentries? Someone will be watching over this place. Overhead vid cams way out here? Terry looked around and up in the darkness. No vidcams.

Wow! The Northern Lights!

She forgot all about where she was and what she was doing, and stared, struck with wonder. When she returned Jess would want to know all about it, so she made up a speech of what she was seeing. "Up in the heavens there was a light show put on by the gods…the northern lights." It had been a long time since she had witnessed this celestial event. Here in Alaska, in perfect darkness without artificial light was ideal for watching the Aurora—if they cared to come down for a visit.

"Torrents of green flowed down like rain shimmering in the wind, sometimes sweeping around in circles half the diameter of the moon. Sometimes they'd become white, red, then blue, teasing the eye, never letting on where they came from or where they were going. They were without start or end. A visual infinity of auroral colored lights roiling and boiling as solar winds buffet our humble little planet."

Jess might even write this down. Her mind continued, 'The lights drizzled down, then whipped like a hose the size of a continent so loudly I could almost hear them. It was a sound of a swish, then a whistle and a snore…'

Snore? The lights don't snore.

She froze, triangulating where the sound of the snoozing was taking place. Focusing on the half-built rock hut nearby she crept up to it. There was a light in the small room where a sentry was probably guarding. She got very close to the window and heard his oblivious slumber. Chancing a wary peek, she leaned into the window and saw the sentry Angel Isaac lying on the floor, sound asleep, beside an AR-15 rifle.

Who was he planning to shoot?

Wielding her knife, she slunk in the doorway, silently reached over, and grasped the rifle by its barrel. She slid it over to her, clutched the weapon and tiptoed away with it.

When she was out of sight, she gave it a quick inspection. Fully loaded with a hundred round clip! She found a rotten log some distance away, rolled it back, placed the rifle under it, and flipped the log on top.

Might come in handy.

She resumed her cruise past the houses. A few had the sound of crying children and two had crying adults. Not the happiest place on earth. The washhouse was empty except for a couple having sex. A few folks still had some energy after a busy day.

Someone's not doing the "One year walk of celibacy before marriage" apparently. A test drive in progress.

Lionel had the luxury of a larger home than the others. Next to his place were rooms for the six Angel Enforcers. It was more of a barracks. Both buildings only had doors facing into the compound. Nobody escapes or sneaks in?

A stealthy stroll by the office revealed a couple of computer monitors brightly lit up and modern public address system lights with what looked like a listening station for the bunkhouses.

Bastards *were* listening in!

No video surveillance because that would have been too obvious, even for them. This place was more and more of a prison camp than religious refuge. Manned, literally and figuratively to what end?

After a round of the south side, barn and workshops she was back in the house with Jess. A good night for surveillance and a bit of future blackmail.

She felt her pocket for the KGB phone and knew she needed to text someone. It had been a gift from a fellow she only knew as The Old Russian. He was a friendly and dangerous operative from the old days. Untraceable even by the KGB.

It was an extraordinary device.

There was no cell service here, but this particular handy phone was not hampered by this limitation. It boasted a dedicated satellite app with no tracing.

Tired, Terry started to put the phone away, had an idea and

resumed texting. "Amelia, check who got big mineral rights in Alaska in the past ten years."

Who were the big fish guiding us small fry?

---

Isaac woke up at his sentry post at dawn. It was the start of another fine day and he already had a good night's sleep while collecting guard pay. He sat up yawning and stretching his arms out. Walt would cut his balls off if he caught him snoozing on the job. So what? The people in the compound weren't leaving, especially after all the bear, wolves and puma scare stories they'd spread.

These city folks were terrified of what lived in the woods.

Once the people got in the camp, they made sure they knew Alaska had thirty-nine mountain ranges, twelve thousand rivers, a hundred thousand glaciers and three million lakes over an area as big as the continental USA. Nobody will find your dead carcass, especially if a wolf pack found it first.

Isaac stood while reaching for his rifle as he stretched once again. The place was empty. Gone? It wasn't in its usual spot. He scrabbled around but could not find it. There weren't any tracks around him. How? Did an animal drag it away?

Panicking, he scrambled around looking everywhere, in the grass and the path that led back to the compound entrance.

What the...?

Isaac wasn't about to say a word about a missing weapon while he was sleeping on the job. He'd have to buy one on his own dime when he was next in Maclean. Hopefully nobody asked to see it until then.

A pretend rubber gun would have to do in the meantime.

---

Des wasn't sure if this new community life was a good idea or not. After two years it consisted of a back breaking cycle of horses, rocks and sleep.

Numbed oblivion.

Des slept like the dead once past the familiar nightmare with the death of his wife. In the past the dream so disturbed him he'd wake up in a sweat and stayed awake for hours. Next day he staggered around, barely functioning. Not a good state for an aircraft mechanic.

This was the first job he really enjoyed after bouncing around barely making ends meet. The stint in Canada was fun but his real reason was dodging his upcoming military draft date. In the end family pressure forced him back twelve hours before they were coming to take him to jail.

In hindsight, the Military was a good move. Des was smart and ended up in the Air force as a mechanic. Five years later he was certified and marketable. Boeing grabbed him and he worked there for almost twenty years. He met Melanie and they were married. They had a child who passed away a year later of cancer. Their medical allowance was cut off shortly afterwards.

Then Melanie got a cancer that ate up their house and savings.

She was in constant pain and convinced him to leave her enough morphine to overdose. In the end, though, she was unable to administer the deadly shot, so *he* did it, much to his never-ending horror and regret. There wasn't a person he knew that didn't hug him and say he did the right thing. It didn't help.

A hollow man.

After that, nightmares kept him awake all night. He lost weight and started making mistakes at work. His colleagues watched him, catching the loose bolts, the missing lock wires and the repair record omissions. His work became so dangerously shoddy nobody would work with him. Miles was a liability waiting to bite them all. Even the union said they couldn't back him anymore.

He drank, smoked pot, experimented with coke in hopes of sleeping. His money gone, he slept in his car in the Boeing parking lot.

His relatives gave up on him. They found him an embarrassing liability. Friends avoided him. They all sympathetically looked the other way. No hope.

His life couldn't have been bleaker. One Sunday morning he awoke hung over and depressed, his back and knees aching from sleeping in his car in a big empty parking lot. His was the only car in five acres of pavement. There was a pamphlet under his only functioning wiper blade.

The pamphlet was a photo of a national park – like setting and the handwritten words:

*Hate your life? Want to get back to the land?*
*Come with us to all God's natural beauty and be with nature.*
*Meet at the old Baptist church 2 p.m. Sunday.*

Miles did hate his life and thought he'd have a look. His wife and little family did go to church each Sunday for a time, though he wouldn't call himself a religious man. Besides, the old church was near the closest, cheapest liquor store.

He dashed into Billy's Booze, spent his last bit of money on a particularly cheap bottle of gin and walked out. It was raining, hard.

"Outta gas!" he cursed as he tried to restart his car. The cops would grab him for drinking in his vehicle for sure. "Frick." He had no money for gas. He noticed the old church was nearby, dry and warm. It had a big "For Sale or Lease" sign out front and looked semi-aban-doned—like his life.

He hated living in the sticky cramped car. With his precious bottle safely under his arm he slipped into the church ten minutes after two. It was half full of people, most listening, a few homeless sleeping in this warm and dry place.

He didn't consider himself homeless because he had a job, though tenuous, and had a car. On the edge.

"Welcome sir! My name is Lionel Garson," the man at the pulpit shouted out cheerfully. "Are you ready to change your life? I was just saying to everyone that 'Motion' is looking for good people such as yourselves."

On the wall behind him he flashed up a massive photo of a scenic, green meadow with mountains in the background. Beautiful. He put up a few more, leaving them up long enough for the people to drink in the beauty and imagine themselves there.

"Do you know what these photo's have in common? We are building farms, back to the land, in each of these locations." He became animated, pointing at individuals in the audience. "You... you could be there right now, in the sunshine, looking over the mountains while tending to your fields of vegetables, hay and livestock. Can you imagine a better place to raise a family?"

The crowd lapped it up. Miles was excited. Escape.

"Is your life worth living if it's in a rat race? All around you there's crime, filthy streets, drug needles abandoned in your only neighborhood park? Are you barely making ends meet? Are you afraid of crime? Tired of breathing smog and car exhaust which causes cancer? You pay every penny you have to hospitals and die anyway. Is that any way to live?"

Some of the group was nodding.

Miles knew what it was like to lose your loved ones and all your money to cancer. He was paying attention.

"Are your kids afraid of crime, drugs and guns in school?"

One man on the left of Miles shouted, "My son got stabbed in school."

"Look at the world. It's full of nuclear weapons, people from other countries sneaking in to murder us in our beds. Remember when they offered you a vaccine to save your life—the price for that vaccine that you be willing to accept a permanent number stamped on your hand? The mark of the devil!"

He paused for effect.

"Now climate change is boiling the world! Look around us. Do you approve of what you see?"

The crowd booed.

"The world will be coming to an end. You can escape all that! Look for yourself! See?" He flashed the photos again. "Go north! Who's with us?"

Half the group raised their hands, including Miles.

"Look at this beautiful picture." Lionel pointed at a place in the photo, then at the first person in the pew. "Would you sir, want to be here?"

The man nodded happily.

"Next to you... Ma'am?" He pointed to another spot in the photo. "You?"

"Oh, yes."

Miles watched as Lionel talked to each and every person attending. Soon the whole church was enthused.

"We have schools taught by scholars and musicians from all over the world. Right now, our churches in England, Canada and America are filling with people just like you. They are shouting out, 'We want to go back to the land and serve our lord!' Are you coming with us?" Lionel shouted.

The group roared, "Yay!"

He pointed to three shabby plywood folding tables to his left and called, "I invite you to sign up right now and be breathing fresh air in a week!"

Lionel skipped over to three tables set up with colourful pamphlets and papers to sign. Six smiling people greeted them, pens, papers and computers at the ready. "Come on over!"

Miles felt tears running down his cheeks. He walked to the nearest trash can and dropped in his unopened bottle of booze. The new group eagerly lined up at the next table, including Miles.

He looked down the string of people and saw well-dressed people, families and a few shabby and homeless like himself. A slice of unhappy humanity.

Someone behind him nudged him forward in the line, a middle-aged man with the name tag 'Roger'. "Name?"

Surprised, he cleared his throat. "Miles Desmond Vickers."

"Place of work?"

"Boeing, twenty-years."

"Ah, let me look you up. Social security number?"

"Um, why?"

The man looked at him helpfully. "We are helping you and you need to help us. The Lord requires half of what you own, including pension and 401k. You'll owe four percent of any future earnings should you leave the camp for any reason."

"Um, seems high."

Roger looked hurt. "Mr. Vickers... Miles?"

"Call me... Des, I guess."

"Des, we are buying this wonderful land and letting you live with us free."

"Sounds fair. Sure, number 354201."

"Gotcha." Roger pulled some pages, ticked some boxes and finally printed out a copy. "...sign here, here, here and here."

"So, I'm signing this over to 'S-GIRP Corp'?"

"Correct."

"And I have to re-apply to get my half back?"

"Yes. You can choose if you wish to get that fifty percent returned subject to a statute of limitations. You can decide then."

"Sounds fair." He doubted any money was left and there were many bills still owing.

"Do you have a passport?"

"Yes."

"You'll need it to go through Canada and on to Alaska. We'll take it from you there."

*Take it from me at the border temporarily or take it forever?*

It was only after a forgettable seventy-two-hour bus ride that he arrived in the town of Maclean's, Alaska. A beefy fellow calling himself a "Guardian Angel" took his passport and threw it into a bag for "safekeeping".

"Don't you want to know my name?" asked Des.

The angel enforcer shrugged.

Here was his chance to let "Miles" and his troubles, bills and personal demons vanish forever. No turning back now. "Then you can call me 'Des'." *Good luck finding me, anyone.*

The enforcer nodded without interest. "Des it is."

That was years ago and here he was, sober, overworked but strangely happier than he'd been since Melanie died. Forty-five years old, anonymous, marooned in a community, penniless, sleeping in a little room in an old army bunkhouse. He sighed and rolled over in his bed.

Des did feel like he had a new lease on life.

---

THE FIRST THING Terry did next morning was to lean into a corner of her bunkhouse and check for messages on her old KGB phone. There were two.

She looked at the long message from Amelia: *"Found this: Mineral rights come with homesteader agreement from the Army Corps of Engineers by Fred Q. Zajac in 1953 for a Pipeline dividend project, no bids, private sale then bought from Zajac by G. Barris for a 'future environmental refuge' complete with army bases, nine years ago. Barris connection to World Oil – Hobson Brothers, who are connected to a little mind control project called MK-Ultra by the CIA. Also connected to Disciples Council."*

Holy moly!

## 9

## LIFE'S A STAGE

"Are you going to write down what I said about the Northern Lights? They were amazing!"

Jess seemed disinterested. "Yes, maybe. We'll see."

Terry was miffed. "Some good prose in there, don't you think? Shimmering and drizzling? Good stuff!"

"I suppose," Jess mumbled as she closed the bunkhouse door behind them. Terry poked a piece of wood shaving into the jamb. "Have your markers moved over the past few days Ms. Spymaster?" asked Jess, glancing both ways.

"Not so far but you never know."

"Time for Sunday morning chow."

Terry's eyes widened in anticipation. "Do they feed us something better on Sundays? Waffles and blueberries?"

"Nope. The usual gruel, half a bun and weak coffee."

Terry winked at Jess. "You'd think the Disciples could afford a better food budget."

Jess's mouth fell open in amazement. She recovered and snapped her head back and forth again before hoarsely whispering, "Disciples? No way!"

Terry just nodded.

After breakfast Terry and Jess moved to the back of the community hall which served as the church. One hundred and thirty-two people filled the crude pews arranged in a semicircle around an area serving as a stage. The seats were packed already. Terry and Jess barely squeezed in at end of the back row. From where they were, the citizens seemed to be looking forward to the work break more than the repetitious Sunday sermon.

Lionel marched out to give the usual zinger opening. "Remember: you are special and here to serve the Lords purpose. Let us pray."

The group bowed their heads.

Lionel announced "We have a special show, today. My wife, Sylvia, has a play she wishes to show us."

Jess was sure everyone around them stiffened or stifled a gasp. "Why's everyone's not looking forward to this?" she whispered to Terry.

They watched Lionel slide his dais out of the way. Jeb and Isaac dragged out two upright poles then settle a cloth-wrapped third pole across the top. A canvas dropped over the front, creating a makeshift curtain.

Jess made a face. "Looks like we're getting a stage show."

"Or a circus. Should be interesting."

After two minutes of Jeb and Isaac fussing with the stage, Lionel stepped in front of the curtain. "And now for the show, 'The Lord Speaks to Us'."

He moved to the left, carefully pulling the big curtain to the side, revealing Sylvia perched on a throne in the middle of the stage. She spoke for a solid minute in some other language or tongues.

"What was that? You're the language person. What language was that?"

Terry whispered back, "Pure gibberish. Seems like something from high school."

Sylvia was still talking. "Om-key ids-kay oot uth-key runt-kay."

Jess watched a dozen kids swarm up to the stage to sit proudly at Sylvia's feet.

"A-Uth-tay B-osen-C-chay D-uns-kay."

Jess leaned over and whispered, "Pig latin-ish...the chosen ones."

"Come to the front kids," Sylvia smugly commanded to those children who had not understood her "weird sounds" instructions. Twenty more children glumly went to the front of the stage to join the "volunteers", some already in tears. Sylvia said, "Welcome to the E-eeds-way."

Jess leaned over, "She called the second batch of kids 'the weeds'."

"I got that."

The audience understood what had just happened. Most were embarrassed while the ones who understood this silly secret language seemed proud and pleased. This performance somehow gave them a better status than everyone else.

Sylvia stood, stepped forward, and lifted her arms to include the adults. "Those of you whose children understood our magic language move to the front. Those whose kids are "Weeds" move to the back."

"Are "Weeds" a bad thing?" whispered Terry, puzzled.

Terry and Jess were already in the rear, and they had no child to classify, so they stayed put. Everyone else moved according to Sylvia's order, the sounds of shifting pews and feet shuffling mixed sometimes with eager talk, more often quiet whispers or mutterings. When everyone had rearranged themselves, about a quarter of the group had set themselves apart on the front, their expressions shining with pride and self-congratulations. Clearly a preferred pecking order had just been established.

Jess shook her head. "This is so cruel."

Lionel returned to the dias and waved his hand at the people in the front of the audience. "Let's have applause for our tongue keepers! Only trust us and our Lord!"

Almost everyone applauded except Terry and Jess. She noticed Des wasn't far from them and he wasn't applauding, either.

Jess whispered, "That's why some of us do the grunt work while the tongue keepers get the cushy jobs."

"Not rock pickers."

NEXT MORNING ISAAC WATCHED TERRY, Jess and Des readying to head out to the fields. He'd noticed none of this team had applauded at the service yesterday. Their poor attitude would be corrected today. He noticed Des was away, getting the horses and the younger rock picker at the washroom so Isaac decided to exert his power starting with Terry. She was alone near the stone boat. Good cover for what he was about to do.

He approached her aggressively. With nobody close by to witness their exchange he could push her around, shout, threaten and make her cry. She might even offer to have sex with him. Bonus. He loved being an Enforcer Angel.

Isaac stormed up to Terry in attack mode. "You! Why did you insult our meeting?"

"Insult?" she asked, her expression unimpressed.

Enraged, he growled, "Yes! You insulted the Tongue Keeper ceremony."

"My bad," she replied, uncaring.

He dashed towards her with his staff like a raging bull. To his surprise she dodged him, tipped him over and rode him down into the rocky ground like a missile. She had his wood staff against the back of his neck, pressing down so hard she was close to snapping it. He froze with fear. Nobody would see this behind the stone boat.

"Isaac, today's your lucky day. I'm not going to snap your fat neck and I won't tell Lionel your pretty AR-15 rifle is missing."

He swallowed.

"A missing rifle from a sleeping sentry. If I'd slit your throat from ear-to-ear, we wouldn't be having this conversation."

He grunted, "How do you know…?" and was rewarded with a mouthful of dirt.

"A sleepwalker I know told me."

Spitting dirt, he said, "What do you want?"

"Back off and leave us alone and nobody will find out what a shitty sentry you are and how you lost your weapon. Got it?"

"Yes."

"Mums the word and you won't have your throat sliced next time. Got it?"

"Yes."

"Clear off and bring us a big jug of drinking water, a bucket and three cups in two hours. Gonna be hot out here."

She helped him stand up and returned his staff. "Beat it. We have work to do." Still spitting dirt, he scurried away like a frightened squirrel.

———

JESS STEPPED over the furrows as she went to the stone boat and saw Terry. Enforcer Isaac had his head bowed in shame. He stumbled and limped past her, face and clothes dirty.

It was a nice day. Terry was throwing rocks into the sled. Des hadn't quite arrived. She heard Des coaxing along the horses from the barns.

Briskly Jess asked Terry, "Why did you beat up the enforcer?"

"He must have tripped."

Jess gave her the look of death.

"He was after me for not approving of the weirdo weed play. You and Des were next."

"We have to keep quiet if I'm going to find my dad."

"I have something on Isaac that will keep him sleeping with one eye open. He's not telling anyone."

"Here comes Des. Good morning!"

He smiled at them like he meant it. "Morning."

Jess watched as Terry took the reins from Des and backed the horse to the hitch to drop in the pin.

They sweated in the morning sun making decent progress not that any of the three cared. Working on the rock pile in a work camp in the middle of paradise.

At nine a.m. sharp a woman came to them with a big jug of cold water, three cups and a bucket for the horses.

Des watched her leave and whispered, "How in the world did that just happen?"

Terry shrugged. "It must have been sent by that humanitarian Isaac."

Jess and Des looked at her in amazement.

The workday went well with a not-bad supper of greasy meatloaf and potatoes.

Terry and Jess walked back from the night's sermon both ready for sleep. A cold-water bird bath served to wake them up, so Jess lay in bed trying to read in the fading light of the midnight sun.

"What are you reading, kid?"

---

THAT NIGHT ISAAC arranged to drive the truck on the next trip to Maclean, their nearest and only town. It was a half hour on the dirt and a half hour on rough pavement. There were always supplies to be picked up. He passed the word with Walt and Lionel he was available to drive.

At breakfast Terry kept an eye on Isaac. She saw by the way he made sure the big truck was fuelled up he was headed for town.

She waited for him at the end of the community hall building, his usual route. As he turned the corner she stepped out, giving him a start.

"Headed to town for a new AR, Isaac?"

"None of your business."

"True. I'd like to go to town, too. I've never been to Maclean. Is it nice?"

"Not really."

"Arrange for me to go along."

"No. Get back to your rock picking."

"I can arrange it with Walt, myself. I'm sure he'd be interested in your sentry expertise, sleeping while someone steals your gun. Resumé material."

She gave him a threatening scowl that made him think she'd maybe break his nose or much worse. He relented. "Alright."

She smiled. "You're a peach."

Isaac took a breath. "We have some stops to make. May and Irene are coming, too. Don't go out of my sight."

"Ah, you angel enforcers make sure 'Only trust us and our Lord' is taking place, right?"

"Something like that," Isaac grumbled. "Meet me at the red truck in the compound in thirty minutes. Don't be late." She had him over a barrel and there wasn't much he could do about it. He wasn't unconvinced she wouldn't kill him in his sleep for the fun of it. In his previous life he'd seen people like her in action. Be afraid.

Best keep his mouth shut until he could find a way to bury this one. She wouldn't be the first.

---

THE RED FARM truck clattered down the dirt road in a cloud of dust with Isaac at the wheel. Terry, May and Irene sat in the open back of the truck on a bench installed for just such a purpose. They all sat together close to the cab to minimize the flying rocks, wayward bees and wasps.

Terry was vaguely aware of May and Irene. They both seemed mildly resistant to the "Motion" crowd. While never standing out they had a little backbone and worked within the system as much as they could. They might have a bit of information to offer.

"You two aren't sitting in the cab with Angel Isaac?"

"Isaac is best left on his own," said May. "He has frisky hands."

"Ah."

"Besides, it's a nice day. You're not riding up there with him?"

"No. Too nice a day," Terry said, wistfully. *And I'd break all his fingers which would be hard to explain.*

May asked, "We noticed you weren't applauding the play yesterday. How come?"

95

Terry measured her words. "I thought the play was mean towards the kids who didn't speak... the Tongue. They're just kids."

May and Irene looked at each other. "We didn't applaud much but enough to keep the Angel Enforcers away. They can be... cruel. Did he come to you?"

"He did." Terry smiled. "We came to an understanding."

May and Irene didn't seem to know what that meant.

"So why did you come here, to the community?" asked May.

Terry had to think of something. "My life was going nowhere, found the Lord and he said go north and pick rocks."

May and Irene laughed, then looked around nervously.

May asked, "Did they recruit you in a Body House?"

Terry was puzzled. "A... what?"

May laughed, grabbing the side of the truck as it lurched over a hole. "Sorry, not a," she spelled it out, "*b-a-w-d-y* house—a *B-o-d-y* House. Different spelling. It's a home that serves as an informal church on Sundays. That's how we got recruited. We got an invite from this nice family who told us about 'In Motion' and here we are."

Irene continued the story, "...and we hated living in east LA. There was no hope then 'Motion' came along. We thought, why not try it?"

"How has it been for you two?"

They looked at each other. Irene confided. "We'd leave if we could, but our husbands would keep our kids. We'd be penniless and homeless and marooned up here. We weren't far from that in L.A."

The old truck clattered and bumped along the narrow dirt road. Isaac couldn't drive very fast.

"Are your husbands both happy here?"

"Yes. They've moved up the pecking order and can do as they please and are now in the local National Guard unit. A bit of power, you know."

"Is Lionel the leader of the community?"

"Six elders are supposed to advise Lionel what to do but it's the other way around."

"Lionel gets his orders from somewhere else and tells Walt to enforce it?"

"Bingo."

"Who tells Lionel what to do?"

"Someone from Florida flies in and lands at the middle community's little dirt strip. Lionel takes the BMW and personally drives to get them and bring them here. Three men with suits and briefcases get out, march into his office, and stay for about two hours. They come out and Lionel drives them over to the other three communities."

"Do they talk to the… citizens or elders?"

"Never. Not even eye contact. We are forbidden to speak to them."

Terry laughed. "So, they're from head office so to speak?"

May and Irene laughed. "Seems that way. That evening, after work, Lionel and Walt get us together and say 'The Lord has come and directs us to…'"

"Ah."

Enough questioning on this trip.

The truck stopped at the intersection, then pulled out on the pavement which was a big improvement in the ride. Isaac hit the speed limit which made talking in the open back difficult.

Terry was enjoying the trip. Everything was green and lush. Periodically they saw a deer or a moose in the ditch.

"Do you ever see bears and wolves?" Terry shouted over the road noise.

May nodded. "I haven't seen them, but Lionel and Walt say the area around the camp is full of them as well as pumas and they will eat us."

"Sure, they will."

The moat was full of alligators, apparently. BS to scare the city folks. Buildings began to appear as signs of a small town grew as they came into Maclean. It turned left and went along five streets, pulling into a building products depot. Alaska Building Supply.

Isaac got out and came around the truck, looking at the trio. "We have some building supplies to get. Here's the materials list. Sign for it 'S-GIRP camp #3'. Keep a copy for the bookkeeper. Get what we need, load it up, and wait for me in the truck."

Irene asked, "Where will you be?"

"None of your fu..!" He caught himself when he looked at Terry. "Um... business. Take your time. There's an ice cream place next door. Knock yourself out."

Terry thought he needs to see someone about a new AR.

The three hopped out and strode to the door. Their sad, long dresses and hats made them stand out like outhouses in a rainy-day parade.

"Is it unusual to be left alone like this, May?"

"No. The Enforcer driver usually goes for drinks. He knows we can't go anywhere. He's more careful with the men. They avoid bringing single people to town because they could make a run for it."

"Does that happen?"

"Occasionally. They just call the local sheriffs who find them and haul them back to the community."

*Wow... the cops are in on this! Good to know.*

Terry, May and Irene shopped around for nails, bolts, paint, two by fours, nail clippers and toilet paper—one ply! It was heaped onto two rolling carts. They signed the bills for it and loaded up the truck.

It was hot and the three headed for the nearby Dairy Queen.

Terry turned away. "I'm going to get a newspaper. Seeing how that evil world is doing these days. See you guys in an hour."

They looked at Terry nervously. May stuttered, "News from the outside world is evil and forbidden."

"I want to see what I'm missing, that's all." Terry marched off.

She could see right away she stood out while walking down the sidewalk in MacLean—it was obvious from the looks she got from the townspeople they knew she was "one of those community folks". It didn't matter. She was headed for the town taxi stand.

Mclean appeared to be quiet and clean. The traffic was deferential to pedestrians and others. Nice place. By the looks of the trucks and business signs it was chiefly in the oil and gas business. Maclean was in the oil rich North Slope. There were giant pipelines to fill such as the Trans-Alaska and Valdez pipelines sending vast amounts to the continental US.

She knew by experience oil money made people rich, crazy and addicted to everything from custom trucks, tattoos, boats, jewelry and cocaine. The self-appointed princes and princesses needed the cash.

As Terry strode nearer to the taxi stand, she heard a familiar sound. An accordion? Sure enough, there was a man...very short with a beard...sitting on a stool with his case open for offerings.

Terry stopped and smiled. "Am I your only audience Gomez?"

"Greetings Major. You are correct. The locals seem to fear me, hence the empty offerings case."

She looked around before speaking. "Meeting at the taxi stand?"

"Yes. It's the one place your fellow community people wouldn't use. Liquor, shopping, food, city hall, police and such. You won't be calling a cab to be taken to the next town three hundred and ten miles away."

"Good point. Did you have trouble getting here?"

"Not really. The Alaska Russia border isn't far. Besides, we used to own Alaska."

"You should have just leased it."

Gomez didn't get the joke.

"Did you get my message?" she asked.

He stopped playing. "I did. You have a strange case going on."

"It isn't a case as much as it's where Jess led me. Her dad is somewhere here at one of the communities."

"Are you sure he's her father?"

"Nope. Now that we're here this whole operation seems peculiar. A dozen of these big communities parked conveniently on the Northern Slope. Oil is everywhere and seems the Hobsons, aka World Oil, made these communities up."

"Why would we care?"

"The Hobsons bankrolled this operation and run it like a corporation while calling it a religious group. There are sixty thousand pliant folks near the few cities up here. They even man the local National Guard."

"Why would the rich Hobsons go through such effort when they could just buy the oil as World Oil?"

"Heard of 'the Council'?"

"No."

"Also known by their strong arm, 'the Disciples.'"

His eyebrows went up and his jaw went down.

"And this is a front for an Alaskan takeover."

Gomez looked at her closely. "A takeover? Wouldn't America rush in and end it?"

"I'm not so sure. Think about it. Alaska is an isolated region. Russia on the north and they'd have to enter through Canada to the south. "

"So, Alaska could become their own Disciples country?"

Terry shrugged. "My suspicious nature."

Gomez had his poker face back on.

She asked. "Could you look up something, occupation aircraft engineer, Boeing. Worked for the US air force as an engine mechanic so you may know who he was. He would have been early thirties in those days and might be living here with us."

"Shall I text you on the special phone?"

"Please."

Gomez resumed playing his accordion. Terry hiked to the truck to catch her return ride to kooky town.

The trip back was very quiet until the truck came upon an accident. A car had struck a deer which lay twitching on the road. There were bits of the car scattered all over, testifying to it having rolled several times, shedding enough plastic and metal to force Isaac to stop.

May looked at the carnage. "Looks like Gary Morse's car. Looks like he was mobile enough to walk home. His place is just over there." She pointed. "Probably getting a tractor to tow this wreck back to his yard."

May, Irene and Terry helped push the crunched-up vehicle to the roadside so their truck could get by. Irene then went over to where the deer lay dying. "Grab a leg!" she called, producing a penknife—a huge surprise—and cut the deer's throat.

The women hoisted the deer into the rear of the truck while Isaac impatiently waited. The trio climbed back aboard, and Irene banged on the cab of the truck to signal Isaac. They resumed their journey.

Terry wrinkled her nose. "Roadkill?"

"Yes. Organically fed deer meat. We'll skip on that beat-up leg, though."

"Ah."

"Really! We don't get much meat, and this is excellent. Remember that meatloaf? If you were a hunter, you'd be looking forward to it and why not?"

"Waste not, want not?"

"Yes. We're ten minutes from the ranch. Guts out and chopped up in an evening."

Terry shrugged. "I suppose."

She hung on to the tailgate as they turned on to the narrow side road that led to the camp. "Is that a river, Irene?"

"It is the Beau River. That's where we get our water and a bit of electrical power. Old army base stuff. See?"

Terry spotted a side dam generator and a telltale heavy black power cable snaking out of the riverbank along the rocks and on to the camp. Probably army issue turbine on the end of a long pipe. Well-hidden on purpose.

---

JESS SAT in the shade wolfing down what was considered lunch today. She envied Terry getting a side trip into the town while she had to stay behind with Des, two stinky horses and two other ladies pitching in, Ann and Pam. Jess said nothing and ate while Ann and Pam gossiped. They were senior camp people.

They talked about kids, weather and God. Suddenly Pam glanced around and whispered to Ann, "Did you see the police dug up Samuel?"

Ann whispered back, "I did... in the rain last week?"

"Yes. It was dreadful."

Jess's ears tuned to the whispers. She held her breath, not missing a word.

Ann and Pam said nothing for a minute, eating and looking around.

Pam added, "That's terrible what they did to Samuel. He was old and a bit senile but quite harmless."

"I agree. I think they just wanted to scare the rest of us."

"They certainly did that. I don't ever want to see another demon exorcism in my life."

Jess swallowed her mouthful of sandwich, hard.

Exorcism?

# 10

# GENERAL TALES

Marjorie: Get me the General Chief of Staff in Washington DC!"
Governor Fairfield commanded.

"General? Chief of...?"

"He's the defacto President of the United States of America!"

"Yes? His name is?"

"No idea. Find him!"

Marjorie grimly picked through a massive official directory for someone called a General Chief of Staff. There was a hundred and fifty pages of various military men running the country these days, all in italicized fine print on poorly printed paper inserts. The directory arrived every three months as the military endlessly changed their people around with the newest royal pecking order, obsolete and incorrect the day it was printed and left Washington, DC.

Paper hell.

She remembered when all this government intrigue started with the arrival of the Hobsons—the richest family in America relocating to the frozen north. It had been a huge deal. Rumour had it, Milton Hobson's wife had made a massive stink about how crappy Juneau Alaska was and how the mansion they were "stuck with" wouldn't be a horse barn back in Wichita. She'd had a complete meltdown hissy fit and was tossing dishes around at a posh welcoming party.

What a bag!

Marjorie would have liked to be there to watch the Hobson's guests ducking and running as priceless crockery was flying. The Governor hadn't duck fast enough and came to work sporting a big bruise on his cheek from an eleven-hundred-dollar Orange-Fitzhugh dinner plate. He'd confided to her that his wife made him sleep on the couch, convinced the injury was from a woman who punched him for grabbing her where she didn't want to be grabbed.

What a crew!

At sixty-six years running, Marjorie was weary of Governor Fairfield's intrigue. Ever since those rich and snooty Hobsons arrived in Juneau, they were constantly meeting with him, making his mind turn this way and that. One of Hobsons PR men came by daily to give the Governor pep talks about what to say and when to say it. Marjorie sometimes brought in coffee and sandwiches and overheard them whispering about millions and billions of dollars changing hands. Alaska was as oil rich as a small Arab country, but the money went into the pockets of only a few Texas oil tycoons, like the Hobsons. The hardworking people up here barely got a sniff.

Just another elite gold rush.

"Frick!" she mumbled to herself as she thumbed through the directory. It was a five-inch-thick block of paper filled with names and numbers jammed into an old black plastic three-ring binder. It was so cheap it wouldn't even stay upright in the bookshelf.

Her assistant Phyllis used to do all the directory updating and other basic functions. Unfortunately, Phyllis was too good looking for her position and the Governor's wife had her fired. Her hemline was too high, her neckline was too low. Damn.

Where should she start?

"You don't need an assistant do you Marjorie?" the Governor asked.

Marjorie kept her curse words to herself and put on her thickest eyeglasses. She started with a random General Tyler McMahon. If they talk to the CIA, Russians, and China, surely they can forward calls down there.

She tried a number. Someone said, "Hello?"

"Hello this is the Alaska Governor's office and I'm trying to find the General Chief of Staff."

A precise military voice chided, "There is no General Chief of Staff, only names, listed last name first with middle initials."

"I know but your directory has pages of generals but..."

"Ma'am I suggest you keep looking through that directory."

Click!

Marjorie took a breath and tried another number, this time for a General J. Smith. "Hello?"

"Yes, General J.J. Smith's office. Can I help you?" said a proper female voice.

"Yes, you can! This is the Governor of Alaska's office and I'm trying to find the General Chief of Staff. Do you know who that is?"

"Do you want General Chief of Staff or the General who's currently the chief of staff?"

"Um, not...sure..."

"Did you look in the latest directory?"

"Um..."

"No? Goodbye..."

"Hold it!" Marjorie was getting annoyed. She didn't get her job by being pushed around by clerk pip-squeaks. "I have the official generals' section in the directory in front of me..."

The receptionist interrupted her. "Are you using directive number 19284-CX-L?"

"I don't know. Let me look at the cover. Um...no, it's CX-K..."

"Sorry, CX-L is obsolete as of the first of May. Goodbye."

The governor's voice shouted at her on the ancient intercom. "Marjorie! Did you find that President General?"

"Not yet sir but soon."

Marjorie could feel her blood boiling and her glasses steaming up. She pushed redial on the last number.

"Hello, General J.J. Smiths office. Can I help..."

Marjorie broke into a barely controlled tirade. "Yes, this is the Governor of Alaska's office, again. The only directory available to me right now has Major Generals, Lieutenant Generals, Surgeon Generals, Surgeon Doctor Generals, Attorney-Generals who were also Major Generals, one through five-star Generals, forty-five Generals named John Smith and forty-nine General Bob Jones, active Generals and retired Generals, Honorary Generals but no General Chief of Staff!"

Peg, the Army receptionist on the line seemed impressed with Marjorie's rant. She gave a good-natured laugh. "Yes, that directory is a mass of generals and they move around every time someone gets a promotion, demotion, or gets fired. Let me look and see if we can find a General Chief of Staff for you." Marjorie heard the sound of papers shuffling, then the tapping of computer keys.

*Please!*

Peg announced, "Aha! The acting Chief is…a General Brant."

"Bless you…," said Marjorie, mopping up a bit of sweat on her forehead with her lace hanky.

"My names Peg."

"Thanks… Marjorie."

"Marj. Try 16537853741, then local 203."

Marjorie barely wrote the numbers all down in time. "Thank you, Peg." *Aha! General Brant! Got you!* Marjorie dialed the long number.

An automated voice replied, "America is Great with your US Military on the ground, in the air, over the water and out in space! Your call is important to us so hold the line…blah…blah…"

"For God's sake…" Marjorie stabbed in a 203 local which made that phone ring.

A voice said, "Chief of Staff."

Marjorie started speaking then realized it was another automated reception which droned on, "…General Gaddy local 900, General Dove local 901, General Eastman local 902…"

The governor barked impatiently, "Marjorie? Where's my General?"

"Um… er… coming sir…"

She ignored him and held her breath as the names and locals droned by for another ten minutes, "...General Brant 973, General Barth 974..."

"973!" she declared, tapping in the extension number.

"General Doctor Brant's office," said a voice.

*Doctor?* She quickly inserted, "This is Governor Fairfield's office. The Governor wishes to speak with General Brant."

"Who's this?" said a surprised voice.

"Governor Fairfield of Alaska needs to speak to the President, General Brant!"

"Ah..." (click – hum)

Did they just cut me off? *Damn!!* Marjorie held the phone, waiting and wondering for five minutes almost crushing the receiver in her old bony fingers.

A gruff voice asked, "Hello?

Marjorie replied, "Hello? Who's this?"

"General Brant speaking. Who are you?"

"Are you General Brant?"

"Yes ma'am."

Marjorie jumped up. "Just a minute general...sorry...Governor, answer the phone!" she shouted, not daring to lose the hard won call on the old switchboard.

"What?" shouted the Governor.

"Answer your phone!"

"What?"

"Answer your bloody phone!" she shouted, immediately regretting it.

---

THIS WAS General Doctor Brant's first day on the job as America's temporary Chief of Staff aka acting president. The top four generals, which didn't include him, each took one month turns at running the country but were unavailable.

"Call for you sir! Line two," called his receptionist, hopefully.

"Me?" Surprised, Brant looked at the ancient army issue phone with all the buttons and mumbled, "God, give me an AR or a rocket launcher and not a fricking phone switchboard."

He looked at all the buttons on the phone and tapped the first one. "Hello?"

Dead. Then he tried the second button. "Hello?"

"Ah…hello?" came a female reply.

"General Chief of staff Brant speaking."

Someone on the line shouted. "Just a minute General… what… Governor, answer the phone… what?… Answer your bloody phone!"

This sounded like picking up the phone at his mother-in-laws house at Christmas.

"Hello?" he asked hopefully.

"Governor Fairfield here, General. Thanks for taking my call."

"Sure, Governor. You are from…?"

"Alaska."

"Ah… let me look at my map, Governor…?"

"Fairfield, sir."

"Fairfield..?

"Governor Fairfield, sir."

"Of course, it is."

"It's an honour to speak to you sir, General Hunt."

"General Hunt? No, I'm acting Chief of Staff Brant. Brant!"

"Ah, are you the …um…president, then?" asked the governor, confused.

"I assure you, Governor, that I am the acting Chief and hence the President."

"Glad to hear it, sir."

Brant thought the governor sounded unconvinced. "It's like this: General Addy and Hunt are away on vacation, General Mills is on medical leave, and General Gerard is on administrative leave."

Brant wasn't going to say the real story that General Mills was getting a vasectomy fixed and General Gerard was under investigation for having sex with General Addy's wife, then tried to shoot them both with General Hunt's gun.

GFU—General Fuck Up, he thought, snorting to himself.

"I see," said the governor, probably wondering what the hell was going on in Washington these days.

Brant thought, and I get to be the "acting" chief because I managed to get into the Ukraine, grab a couple of atomic bombs General Addy managed to lose in Turkey and brought them both home without any shooting—thanks to that warrior princess Major Reid and fifteen cases of Kentucky bourbon. *I'm definitely not going to tell you that, Governor.*

"Well Mr. President…er …General…"

"Call me Doctor Brant. I'm a Psychiatrist."

There was a pause on the phone. "The President is 'a shrink', sir?"

"Why yes." Brant replied proudly. He thought, we wouldn't be in this mess if we had a shrink running the country twenty years ago.

The Governor paused, then moved on. "I won't take up much of your time Dr. Brant. I was wondering—how many troops do you have posted in Alaska these days?"

"That's a random question Governor."

"Yes, well… er…"

"Expecting an invasion Governor?"

"Um… not generally, sir."

"Are the penguins getting restless?"

"We don't have penguins here General."

"I know… a little joke, Governor."

The governor managed a squeak of a phony laugh.

"You need some troops?"

The governor sounded nervous. "Uh, no sir. The little towns near the bases like the troops around as it's good for business but bad for law enforcement."

"You know the army, Governor… boys will be boys… blowing off steam and all that."

"How many troops, sir?" the Governor persisted.

Brant looked at his wall display. "I'm looking at my map and not seeing many of our troops up there, sorry. Overseas commitments are piling up. We can hustle in a mobile force in a few planeloads and choppers if you're in a hurry. More efficient."

Actually not, but it sounded good.

"Depending on the weather?"

"Yes, depending on your famous Alaskan and west coast weather," Brant added.

"So, you have… how many?"

"Expecting an attack any moment, Governor?"

"Um… no. Just asking."

"It looks like we have about two-fifty, mostly admin staff and a few National Guard instructors. You have about five hundred National Guard troops and a few bush pilots."

Barely a skeleton force up there thanks to ass-kissing the Russians these days.

"Good, thanks Dr. Brant. Have a good day, sir."

"You too Governor… Hadland?"

"Fairfield, sir…Fairfield."

"Ah, of course it is." Brant hung up, shaking his head thinking 'Mobile Force H' was all he had at his disposal these days. Everyone else was committed to fighting their many enemies all over the planet. This is how it is when you spurn your friends and allies.

Perturbed by these thoughts he dialed a number.

"Joint Chief of Staff, Admiral Lowry speaking."

"Norm! How's it going?" asked Brant.

"Fine Dr. Brant, sir."

Brant liked his Vice Chief. He was efficient yet candid about the state of the military. A no bullshit guy.

"Norm, how's the naval availability these days?"

"Same as last week, sir. All the nuke ships are in port."

Brant sighed in defeat. "Still having technical troubles with the reactors?"

"Yes. We can't seem to get them running sir. Old complex iron and nobody knows how to keep them operating."

"How about the larger conventional ships?"

"Same problem as before, sir. Virus! When we squish more than two hundred men on a ship and take it to sea, the fricking 'B-walk-4' virus makes them all sick in a few days and the cruise is over. Subs are the worst."

"Damn. Like the Norwalk virus on cruise ships?"

"Yes sir, except we can't get rid of it. Close quarters without windows makes the men violently ill. The men are fine after a couple of weeks if they can stay in the fresh air, but it takes a month to clean the ship afterwards."

"At least we can spread the troops out. It makes them better targets, unfortunately."

"Are the medical teams getting any closer to a fix for B-Walk-4?"

"They think it's a mutation of the old Covid20 but triggered by motion sickness. *One* man pukes and *every* man on board is puking and shitting. Same for troops on crowded planes. They're suffering after a few hours. We can only have two-hour flights, so you can skip any ideas of troops going to Hawaii, Guam and Alaska."

"Jeez."

"Besides, the runways at all the Alaska airbases are dug up for renovations and resurfacing."

"*All* of them?"

"Yes, sir. We're mid-project as we speak. Some huge deal. Couldn't wait."

"Bad plan. Any closer to a virus solution?"

Norm complained, "We don't have many scientists these days, sir, and other countries won't work with us. They're calling all our ships the USS BarfinShit."

"Assholes!" Brant took a deep breath. "We're getting what we deserve after abusing our allies all these years. Denmark hates us, England hung up on me, yesterday, and Canada posted troops at border entries. How do you piss off Canada?"

"We wrote the book on that, apparently. I knew it was the end when Canada stopped sending us the Christmas tree for Boston."

"I saw that."

"Sad, sir."

"Keep up the good fight, Norm."

"Yes, sir."

Brant hung up and leaned back in his chair, deep in thought. Sliding forward, he looked at the confidential phone in front of him and dialed a number. Someone picked it up on the first ring.

"FBI, Acting Director David Bradley speaking."

"Director Bradley, this is General Brant, Acting Chief of Staff calling. How are you?"

---

DAVID BRADLEY WAS glad to have a proper and professional headquarters again. It wasn't the largest building around, but it was secure, and Flo was thrilled they'd gotten a lot of their technology back. He had a staff of almost two hundred, kept busy constantly.

The days of being banned because you were black seem to be going away.

"I'm good, General Brant! So good to speak to you. Acting President?"

"Yes, well, everyone else went on holidays... sort of."

"I'm sure you're the best man for the job, sir. How can I help?"

"I have an odd request. Are you aware of any funny business going on in Alaska?"

"Funny business, sir?"

"Yes. I just got a call from Governor Fairfield, I think, and he made a huge deal to find out how many troops we have up there."

"Like asking how many guards will be at the bank Tuesdays and Thursdays?"

"Yeah—like that. I told him we have very few except for the National Guard."

"Yes. Is there anything... new?"

"I heard the tycoons, the Hobsons of World Oil, suddenly moved up there. A group of communities are trying to cash in on some old oil leases with abandoned army bases on top of them."

"Communities?"

"Some sort of a cult thing. They have a dozen, mostly near a little backwater town called Maclean. Back to the earth and such."

"Do you have any FBI staff in Maclean?"

"No, we don't at this time. Should we, sir?"

"I'd like to see it."

"Yes sir," answered David.

General Brant continued, "I was wondering if you could imbed a couple of trusted men in and around the place—strictly on the down-low. Got any ex-militaries?"

"I could, sir. You want them sent up as civilians? Perhaps they could join the local National Guard?"

"Good idea. Can you do that?"

"It shall be done."

"I'll have Colonel Yearwood e-mail you the details of what I need to see," said the General.

"Very well, sir."

David Bradley hung up the phone and started to grin. He called out, "Flo? Do you have a number for Dean and Trev, the 'Royal Security Twins'?"

# 11

## ROYAL BLISS

The security man stood in his three-piece suit near the exit of a particularly nice hotel. There was no bad news so far. That wouldn't last.

"Sir, Royal Prince Edward III just drove off with Princess Anne's Range Rover. Is he old enough to drive?" asked the valet sheepishly to the royal security man.

"No! That little turd's no prince and he's only fourteen!" the tall, older man hissed in return.

The valet looked concerned. "What shall I do, sir?"

"Give me a minute..." He turned away and stomped over to a second man.

"What's up Dean-O?"

"I hate these kids, Trev! I hate the parents, too. Spoiled, snotty nosed royal..."

"Easy. That's technically the parent's car and they *are* royalty."

"I don't *care* if he's some runaway royalty's kid—*he doesn't* have a driver's license. What do you want me to do?"

Trev took a breath. "I don't know... call the sheriff?"

"Just fricking dandy. I hate this job. The Bradleys said this would be a soft touch."

"I'm not a fan, either. David Bradley said this was a high priority."

"How did we get this, anyway?"

Trev snorted. "They asked you and you said you'd be pleased and honored...a pleasure to assist the FBI in their security efforts—"

"Shut up!" Dean brushed him off. "I changed my mind."

Undeterred, Trev continued, "You also said, 'That would be fun. Pay is decent, home every night, soft touch, yes, your highness—'"

"Shut up! What's the number for the sheriff?"

Trev's phone lit up. "Call for you, Dean. It's David Bradley. Take it and I'll call the sheriff."

Dean shook his head then took the phone from Trev. "Dean here."

"How are you doing?"

"I've had better. Why?"

"If you're tired of royal security I have something else for you and Trev."

"We'll take it."

"Aren't you going to ask what it is?"

"Nope."

"We have a couple of Renta-cops coming to take over from you tonight. Come see us tomorrow morning at the office at eight. Tell Trev."

"Shall do!"

⸻

TREVOR RESER STOOD with Dean Williams and Joyce Carson in front of David Bradley's desk at the new FBI headquarters in Washington DC.

David suggested, "Grab a coffee and sit down, everyone."

Soon all three were huddled around the table looking at David Bradley. What was this all about?

"I had a request from the acting president, a General Brant. He said there are some odd goings on in Alaska and wants an FBI representative—that will be you, Joyce—to go to Maclean. He also authorized two positions for National Guard instructors. That's Dean and Trev."

Eyebrows went up.

"General Brant? I thought it was Hunt or Addy or some other General running things?" asked Joyce.

David took a deep breath. "It's been a gong show ever since Terry put away the head of the CIA and the military get to be president. Truth is, the generals hate the job and are down to playing hot potato with it and juggle it around a group of them."

"A general committee of generals?" asked Trev.

"Would appear so. An order from anyone of those is the word from God."

"Haven't we heard that one before?" said Trev, seriously.

David nodded. "Yes, we have. You three will travel as civilians by car through Canada and arrive in Maclean in six days."

"That's a long drive through a big country," said Joyce.

"That's why all three of you go together and split the driving. Beautiful country. Tell the border people you all have jobs to go to. We'll supply documents. Trev and Dean are airbase workers and National Guard instructors on the side."

"Drill sergeants? Cool!" grinned Trev.

David ignored the comment. "And Dean will be a Captain and Trev senior Lieutenant."

"Salute me Trev!"

"That'll be the day."

David gave them an annoyed look. "Your papers are in the envelope in front of you. Old school, no e-mails. Keep this quiet. You are to be watching while you are up there.

"Joyce, you walk into the Maclean Sheriff's Office, unannounced, like you own the place. Take the designated FBI office. Get a feel for what's going on."

"It has an FBI office?"

"Yes, and a part-time officer, but we haven't heard from him in almost nine weeks. He does his own thing—this isn't unusual for him —does a bit of trapping on the side. He's an odd guy, even for the FBI."

"Is the sheriff's office concerned about him?"

"Not in the least."

"Dysfunctional sheriff's office part two, here I come. What's this agent's name?"

"We inherited him. His name's Jason S. Bemon. A local part-timer we picked up. Goes by his middle name up there... um... Samuel."

# SIX LONG DAYS ON THE ROAD

"They only gave us six days to get from Washington DC to Alaska? Did they even look at a map?" groused Joyce as she put her three suitcases in the back of the green military Ford van.

Trev snorted. "We're Americans. We can barely find America on a world map let alone anywhere else."

She watched Dean heap his luggage on top of everyone else's. He barked, "So let's go. Times a-wasting."

They piled in with Joyce driving and Trev operating the big folding map. Dean wrangled their coffees as the van lurched around corners and edged on to the freeway.

"Got a route for us, Mister Paper GPS?" she asked.

"Um, I think so. It's a perfect route not counting road construction and accidents."

Trev turn the big paper map sideways.

Dean suggested, "Two hour driving shifts each for a twelve-hour day?"

"Works for me."

"Two days into this and I'm liking the scenery up here. This place is called…?" asked Dean.

"Muncho Lake. It's very cool."

"Four days to go and we're in Maclean, Alaska."

---

Cameron, the Maclean Motor Motel owner, sized-up the three people standing before him. They looked like military types. Standing straight, crisp haircuts, polite and direct. The camo van they'd rolled up in didn't mean much around here—camo or faded green was the preppers preferred paint job when the world ends.

"We need three rooms for two weeks. Got something close together?"

"Sure. Sign here and here."

"Will you take an Army charge card?"

"As long as it pays in real money," he grinned.

*I wonder why they're here?*

---

At Maclean's World Oil office Dean finished filling in his employment records form and signed it. He looked over at Trev. "Done?"

"Yup. I'm the new star employee of 53674 Corp–Airport Construction Division/Alaska. How about you?"

"Ditto. I'm actually looking forward to doing something other than royal security and driving. Pay's decent."

"Me too. That was a long drive. Great scenery, though."

"Looks like the supervisor is coming."

---

Dan Wilson had worked at the MacLean Airfield for twenty-nine years. Getting two new workers was a pleasant surprise. They looked like they could walk and chew gum at the same time—a bonus up here.

"Dean and Trev? Got your lids and safety stuff? Good, follow me and we'll take that pick-up to the work site. You two willing to work?"

They nodded.

"Most of the people we get are here to make the magic oil money for standing around and picking their noses. Fired lots of them."

The two men looked back at him in tandem and smiled. What were these two up to? No time to find out.

They climbed into a beat-up Ford pickup with Dan. He gave his new employee speech as he drove. "My name is Dan Wilson. I'm a fulltime farmer working here fulltime to pay for it. Welcome to '53674 Corp'. We're a subsidiary of World Oil. We keep this US Air Force runway at Maclean ready for action. Hours are eight to four each day, coffee at ten and two-thirty with a thirty-minute lunch. Phones off and in your pockets or I throw it under the excavator. Any questions so far?"

The two men shook their heads.

"Our project is to dig up the runways and replace all domestic water and sewer piping, fire system with other trenching for electric trunk lines feeding the runway lights. After that it has to be repacked and repaved. Huge deal. We'd be lucky to finish the early dirt work before the snows fly—*if* we had full staff and all the equipment— which we don't. Paving will be happening next year."

Trev asked, "Are the runways useable while we do this?"

"Nope. This same project is being done on every airfield in Alaska. I think they'll be dead for two, possibly three years."

Dean asked, "World Oil doing runway work?"

"All these runways up here need a couple of thousand tons of asphalt for these multilayered surfaces. World Oil wants to get in on it and the governor agreed."

"The governor and World Oil are in tight?"

Dan smiled. "Governor Fairfield and the Hobson brothers are best buds." He drove from the fenced yard and pulled on to the deserted runway. Here he floored it and soon they were traveling at ninety miles an hour. He smirked. "No planes on a runway and I can drive as fast as I want. Assuming I don't crash into those big honking trenches we dug. See over there? Those are Ken's excavators. He's okay. Never says much, which is good."

The pickup stopped at the edge of the big trench. They got out and Dan led them to the edge. It was long and deep with loose gravel crumbling down to the bottom. It smelled of ancient clay and jet fuel.

"Ken's the boss. Harry, Blaine and James are operating the hoes. You guys climb into the trench and dig around the pipes when the hoe bucket gets close. The pipes are in perfect condition and we want to save them. Got it?"

They nodded.

"See the big metal spreader down in the trench? That's called shoring. It keeps the trench from caving in and killing you. Don't go down there without shoring in place. Digging your dead carcass out afterwards is a time waster and paperwork generator. Watch out for the machinery. Got it?"

More nodding.

"And that's where your phones go if I catch you using them during work hours. I hate phone time wasters. See the guy with the blue hardhat in that Case? That's Ken. Wave."

Ken looked at Dan and gave him the finger.

Dan laughed. "Ken's the chairman of the welcoming committee. Bye." He jumped into the truck and drove away, foot to the floor. He needed two hundred men on this runway job—he had five.

Dean and Trev watched Dan's pick-up speed away. They stood like wall flowers at the dance for several minutes while the machines relentlessly dug in the huge trench.

"You two! Get down there and shovel off that pipe," called Ken.

"That'd be us," said Dean, grabbing a shovel and sliding into the trench with Trev following. They quickly uncovered the pipe enough for the big Case hoe to move along.

"So, the Hobsons of World Oil got together with the governor to paralyse all the asphalt airbases in Alaska at once. Nothing big gets in or out." Dean frowned.

"No landing lights at night so no choppers either," noted Trev.

"Alaska is on its own if things get exciting," nodded Dean. "Whose bright idea was this?"

"Hey! Get digging you two!" shouted Ken.

"That'd be us, again."

---

JOYCE CARSON DROVE her van to the front of the MacLean Sheriff's office. She was dressed in her regulation American FBI agent uniform right down to her gun, knife and handcuffs. She had the official socks, too!

The look of the place reminded her of the bad old days in Washington, being pushed around and bullied by the men when she was a lowly deputy searching for Verbeeldings with Terry Reid. She took a breath and headed for the building's door.

She'd read David Bradley's briefing notes twice, thoroughly. He listed what their FBI office contained, the type of official car, and what part of the main office's heat, light and rent they covered. Joyce wondered what Jason S. Bemon, aka Samuel, was like or where he would be. Was he around? Quit?

Joyce burst through the office door like she owned the place.

"Stop! Who are you?" demanded the receptionist at the desk near the door. According to her name tag she was 'Sally' and she was chewing a piece of gum like her life depended on it.

"I'm from the FBI. Agent Carson. Here are my credentials." Joyce loved flashing her badge while keeping a stone face. She'd practiced in the mirror for hours. Once and a while she'd say "Bond, James Bond" for a laugh.

Sally looked at her, beating up her gum a few more times. "FBI?"

Surprised, Joyce repeated. "Federal Bureau of Investigation."

"Ah. Ya mean like Samuel?"

"Uh…yes."

"Well. He ain't here, so ta speak."

"Oh. Then let me speak with your sheriff."

"Ya mean Abe? He's gone for the day." Sally gave her the fish look, mouth open and stared at Joyce with unblinking eyes. She remembered the gum and started chewing furiously again.

Joyce was stalled out. "I'll use the old FBI office Samuel's using."

Sally gummed a few more times. "Sure, but ya won't like it in there."

Joyce was getting peeved. She represented FBI G men… and a few women… all over America. Who was this gum chewer?

"Let me see that office!"

"Okay, follow me." Sally flipped her bleached hair back while keeping her eyes on Joyce and sashayed into the hallway. She was in her mid-twenties, was short, thin and having trouble walking in a pair of worn spike heel shoes.

Joyce noted first the location of the sheriff's office then two doors past was a similar-sized office. A piece of cardboard was taped in the window—*Morgue*.

"Here ya go!" Sally took some small pleasure in her big reveal.

*Morgue?* Joyce stood in the doorway disgusted. Was that formaldehyde she smelled? Two small desks were in the middle of the room, joined by a stained seven-foot-long slab of green countertop. It had a peculiar stand on one end.

"What the… ?"

Sally ripped the cardboard proclaiming "Morgue" off the translucent window, revealing "Federal Bureau of Investigation – Maclean Alaska" beneath. "Let me know if ya need anything. The washroom is back and to the left. We have ta use the men's so make sure ya lock your stall if the guys come in. They just keep pushing stall doors until they find one open."

"Elegant. When's Samuel returning?"

"I heard them saying he's dead but better to ask Rick. I think he was cutting him up on your desk." Sally snorted with laughter and clumped away.

Joyce called after her, "Who's Rick?"

"The coroner. He's a vet."

"Ex-Army?"

"Yup. Ex-Army vet *and* the local veterinarian. Critter doc!"
*The last FBI agent was cut up on that desk by a vet?*

---

DEAN AND TREV worked up a sweat as they shoveled their way along the pipe in the trench.

Dean didn't mind the project. The hoe would dig away the main trench, Ken moved the shoring along to where they worked, and Trev and he would shovel the last bits so the machine didn't damage the pipe.

Ken shouted down to them. "No need to be too careful with that pipe 'cuz we're putting in new ones."

What? Not according to Dan…

---

JOYCE DROVE to the "Cats to Cows Veterinarians" clinic in her rental car. Once inside, she flashed her FBI credentials to the vet tech and asked for Rick Forest. The effort seemed lame in a critter clinic.

The tech wordlessly pointed to a chair and picked up the phone.

The seven people in the waiting room stopped speaking and looked at her in vague surprise. A cat leapt out of a woman's arms and was immediately chased by some fellow's big black dog who wanted to play. The cat did not, latching its claws onto the big friendly dog's head. The dog screamed and ran while the owners chased.

Joyce took a deep breath and waited in the din of shouting, swearing, cat hair, barking and dog slobber.

Maybe she should wait in her car.

A big, older man in a green medical smock and dripping long rubber gloves came out to her. "I'm Rick Forest. I'd shake your hand but I'm up to here in a cow."

She could barely hear him over the ruckus from the dog and cat running around the waiting room, the cat lady screaming at the dog owner who repeated, "Billy-Bob, come! Billy-Bob, come!"

Rick looked around and said to Joyce, "Follow me to a quieter spot. You can talk to me while I work. I have a calf stuck in the cow and it can't wait. Don't usually deliver here at the clinic, but this little lady's special. Critter midwifery."

Joyce shuddered to herself but agreed and followed him into the back of the concrete block shop. She'd seen it all as a former deputy.

The sound of the cow bawling got louder and louder.

"So, Mr. Forest, you are the coroner?"

"Call me Rick and yes I've been the regional coroner for ten years."

"I think your morgue is set up in my office."

"I suppose, eh...here's my cow. Stand back. I can answer questions as I work."

Joyce was a city girl without farm experience, but she could see how distraught the cow was and felt badly about taking Rick away from his efforts. She watched in horror and amazement as he reached deep into the cow, skillfully manipulating the calf in his efforts to save both the calf and cow. There were grunts, splats, gurgles and dribbles and the little calf was finally pulled out, bawling, which was so touching it almost brought her to tears.

What's that awful smell?

Then Joyce threw up.

---

Trev opened his lunch bag wondering what was in there. He and Dean simply asked the hotel restaurant to make them a bag lunch and hoped for the best. Two sandwiches, an apple and a can of Coke. Was that blueberry pie? Not bad.

They sat on the running boards of a hoe which gave them shade, away from the others. They were just the labourers, apparently. "Go eat there."

"How do you suppose Joyce is doing?" Trev asked as he pulled a bit of meat out and yanked off a shard of gristle.

Dean shrugged. "She wasn't looking forward to a sheriff's office. Bad memories in Washington."

"I'll say. She and Anna had a terrible time with those corrupt deputies."

"That did build her confidence and they won't be able to push her around anymore. Terry showed her a useful move or two. She'll be fine."

"I'm sure Joyce is sitting in her new FBI office going through her files and sharpening her pencils."

———

RICK SAW Joyce was looking woozy, teetering around and throwing up. It never occurred to him that standing in a pool of cow urine, poop and god knows what would be tough for the uninitiated.

"Sorry!" Rick grabbed her so she didn't topple over into a pool of something nasty and steered her to the door. "Marion! Can you take the cow from here?"

His tech confirmed, "Yup, got it Rick."

As he steered Joyce out he realized he was holding her up with his filthy rubber gloves getting cow poo and pee etc. on her FBI uniform. *I won't mention it unless she does.*

He sat her down in their little coffee room, away from the patient rooms and surgery. The little electric ceiling fan seemed to help her while he slid his gloves and smock off and put them in a plastic bag.

"Are you okay Joyce?" He offered her a cup of cold water.

"Ooh. Yup. Thanks."

The water perked her up. "Wow, I've never felt faint before, except for a scene with old bloated bodies." She regretted the thought of the motel in the Verbeeldings case which almost made her barf again. Another gulp of water held it down.

Deep breath.

"This isn't the best place to talk, Joyce. Come and have dinner with my wife and I tonight...6 pm...223 Presidents Road. We're the ones with the white fence and two metal horses at the gate."

Joyce nodded and Rick left. She wearily got out to her car and climbed in. It was hot from sitting in the sun.

What was that awful smell?

---

WENDY FOREST GREETED Joyce at the door of their home. Sluggo, her Jack Russell Terrier started barking.

The woman smiled and said, "I'm Joyce Carson. Rick invited me over for dinner."

"Call me Wendy. Come on in. Ricks still at work but won't be long. Calving season is always a huge deal."

"Thanks."

"Wine or tea?" asked Wendy. The dog barked and tried to nip at Joyce's feet. "Sluggo! Behave!"

"Tea is fine." Joyce looked down at the growling Terrier. "Does Sluggo bite?"

"Yes. Just ignore him; Rick does."

Joyce followed her into the living room. Wendy brought in the tea.

"Rick doesn't like your dog?"

"No. Sluggo and I came as a matched set. He won't even let Rick sit beside me on the couch, so we usually have to lock him up. I'm sure he'd poison him in a heartbeat if I wasn't watching. A vet with a crabby dog doesn't look good."

"Ah."

"Changing the subject, you're dressed very nicely, Joyce."

"Thank you. All my other clothes are in the wash after my calving experience."

Wendy laughed hard. "Calving is *so* messy. I think Rick let me watch so he could see if I was a fussy city girl or not. It's interesting from an obstetrics point of view but gross! I threw up even though I'm a medical doctor myself. Did you barf?"

"Watching the little calf stand up and start mooing was touching but I threw up when the smell got to me."

"Rick likes to break new folks in. So, you are the new FBI agent for Maclean?"

"I am."

Wendy went quiet, sipping her tea.

Joyce spoke up. "Did I say something wrong?"

Wendy shook her head. "Are you hear to find out what happened to Samuel, your predecessor?"

Joyce wrinkled her eyebrows. "I will eventually. Why?"

"Rick had best tell you all about that."

That sounded ominous.

A truck door slammed then the back door of the house opened and closed. Sluggo broke into a furious barking fit and ran towards the noise.

"Beat it, Sluggo!"

"Rick?" Wendy called out.

"Yes, let me shower and I'll be there in fifteen! Come here Sluggo… into your kennel…ouch!"

"Got it," Wendy answered. "Nobody gets in without Sluggo's knowing about it."

An awkward silence followed as Wendy thought she'd said too much and Joyce wondered what she meant.

Joyce broke the silence. "I was surprised the town coroner was a veterinarian. That's unusual."

"It is. He picked it up when he was between wives. I'm wife number five," Wendy said proudly with a touch of sarcasm.

"Number five?" Joyce broke into a grin. "*There's* a business card slogan for you."

Wendy smiled too. "I suppose."

---

DEAN AND TREV walked into their shared hotel room. It had been a long day. Dean showered while Trev picked through their phone messages.

"Hey guys, this is Joyce. Got a dinner engagement. Could you get my clothes from the laundry before you go out? Furthest left dryer, below the bear poster. Got covered with cow crap at the vet's. Long story. Thanks."

Joyce's first day sounded more interesting than theirs had been.

---

TERRY SENSED the buzz of excitement at the Sunday breakfast table. Something was happening. She whispered to Jess. "What's with all the army uniforms? Attacking someone, today?"

Jess shook her head. "National Guard Unit practice apparently."

Terry was excited at the prospect. "Running into the woods to throw grenades, have target practice, repel from helicopters in the sky?"

"Nothing like that. All they do is practice marching in the town square for a couple of hours while Jeb and Isaac yell at them."

"Do they get guns?"

"Just uniforms, a hat and boots."

Terry snorted. "Just as well. They might shoot the angels and take over this place."

"Probably crossed their minds."

"Ah, just manly-men marching aimlessly and harmlessly?"

"Pretty much. They don't seem to mind because it means no chores for the morning. A bit of a spectacle."

"When does it start?"

"A truckload of instructors comes in from the airfield and they show them what to do. Jeb and Isaac are just side shows."

"Do we get to watch?"

"No. Des is marching around too, so you get to run the team and I get to pick the rocks."

"Crappy deal. Maybe you and I should learn to speak in tongues for that play and get a better job around here."

"Unlikely. Gotta go, Auntie. You need to get the horses, remember? Des won't be here and it's seven o'clock."

"No speech from Lionel about 'Only trust us and our Lord' and such?"

"Skip it. The square is busy."

"Army before God? Seems weird for them."

"It is. Horses?"

"Oh yes. The big barn in the north end?"

"Yes. Meet you there."

Terry made a face, skipped the sad coffee, and headed for the exit. The best part of her day was the walk to the field. The weather was cool as the sun peaked over the hills and crawled up in the wide blue sky.

The horses in the barn were glad to see her. She tacked them up with the harness as Des had shown her. She followed behind holding the reins as they clip clopped down the trail towards Jess and the stone boat. Terry was almost content.

———————

"LET'S GO PEOPLE!" shouted Dan Wilson. "We need to be rolling in five minutes to make it to the east community in time! I'll drive, Rick's riding shotgun. You two ok to snuggle in the back?" Dan smiled. Army humour.

Dean stood straight. "I'm the ranking officer here, Willson."

Trev, Rick, Dan all stood at attention and saluted. "Yes Captain."

Capt. Dean barked out, "Lieutenant Willson drive, Lieutenant Forest ride shotgun and Lieutenant Trev and I to snuggle in the back seat."

Same thing.

They barely covered their smirks. "Yes sir."

More Army humour but with proper top-down authority.

They assumed their positions and headed down the paved road from the airbase. Dean leaned over the seat to Rick and Dan. "I take it the road isn't paved all the way."

Rick answered. "No sir. This is all we get for pavement. Thirty minutes of bumpy dirt coming up."

"Do we practice like this every Sunday?"

"We only come when they request it. Technically they are a National Guard unit and we are the 196th Army Reserve Instruction. Different outfit."

"They do their own thing, generally?" asked Dean.

Rick looked at Dan then back to Dean. "Permission to speak freely."

"Of course."

"The communities only march around, every Sunday, unarmed. They have rubber guns. No real weapons allocated. No manoeuvres or schemes. They never leave the parade square. They only ask us if they can't do something, like marching."

"A glorified cadet group but for adults?"

"Yes sir. Show and exercise."

"Do they have their own Non-coms?"

Dan shook his head. "They have three, 'Angels' they call themselves, who are just annoying local goons. Lionel is their sergeant we never see."

Dean was silent. "Is there a purpose for this National Guard unit? Units?"

"Don't know. A year ago, the governor decided each community would have a unit...a hundred in each...four hundred troops in all."

Dean grimaced. "What does a cult need with four hundred unarmed troops who can only march?"

Trev spoke up, "To parade down a street to impress everyone."

Dan pointed out, "Community entrance coming right up."

---

AN ARMY Suburban truck was going to intersect Terry's path, forcing her to stop. Being creatures of habit, the horses were unhappy with this unscheduled event. They dithered back and forth, skittish and bouncy while Terry hung on to the reins.

"Easy boys...wait for these army knobs to get by," she soothed.

The truck slowed trying not to annoy the horses any more than they had to. A couple of the passengers sure looked familiar. Not possible, way up here.

The vehicle continued to the marching square area while Terry stood, deep in thought.

---

DAN DROVE the truck through the main gate of the community, between the big stone fences.

Trev remarked, "Classic 1960's army compound."

Dan added, "…and on the left is a horse team from the 1800's."

Rick pointed to the team. "Watch you don't spook those horses, Dan."

They all gawked to the left, watching a woman struggling with a pair of horses, one frisky and the other bored, barely keeping them off the road.

"Come on lady… keep those hay burners to the side!" groused Dan, dodging them while trying not to bump the entrance way stones.

Dean and Trev watched the horses and the driver. *Was that Terry?*

Trev glanced at Dean who put a finger to his lips and barely shook his head. *Silence!*

Dean's mind raced with questions. Why is Terry Reid running a team of horses in Alaska in a weird-o community?

The truck arrived at the parking lot and the four men piled out.

"Dan and Rick go ahead," Dean ordered.

Trev looked at him and whispered, "Ter…?"

Dean nodded. "Must be some secret thing so say nothing."

"Why is she here?"

"If Terry's here the Disciples are near."

# 13

## MARCHING BADLY

Sergeant Walt and Corporals Isaac and Jeb stood on the side of the main camp square anxiously watching their national guard unit assemble. A crowd of wives who had no assigned duties brought their bored children to watch and quietly heckle.

Jeb watched the spectators and suggested, "Shall I run off the look-ers, sir? They were damn annoying last time."

Walt shook his head. "No, let them watch. Hopefully these new instructors will make this marching practice go smoother than the last few sessions."

Jeb added, "They looked like a herd of deer running around a busy highway."

Walt gave him a dark look. "You guys are supposed to be showing them what to do! I don't think you know your left from your right. Idiots!"

Jeb, Lionel and Isaac slouched in embarrassment.

Walt noticed a vehicle approaching. "Hey, the army guys are coming. Look alive you two! We need this crowd to be able to march into town and scare the shit out of the citizens when the day comes."

The army suburban rolled to a dusty halt at the edge of the square and four impeccably uniformed men got out.

DEAN SMARTLY MARCHED DAN, Rick and Trev over to where locals Walt, Lionel, Jeb and Isaac stood. Trainers meeting the trainees. It was meant to be a show as well as be intimidating. Army logic.

"Halt!" Senior Lieutenant Trev announced.

There was an awkward silence and a few smirks from the 'Angels'.

Trev got in their faces, barking at them, "Where ARE your salutes? Attention!"

Shocked, Walt, Jeb and Isaac jumped but only managed sloppy salutes.

"That is *no* salute! This is how YOU salute, soldier!" Trev barked, demonstrating a salute. "You are a SOLDIER today, not a frigging farmer!"

Irritated and embarrassed, the trio stood holding their modified salutes.

While Trev berated them, Capt. Dean surveyed the bedraggled parade square—scattered rocks, a half rotten log, tufts of wild, unmowed grass, a half dozen piles of fragrant horse poop, a solitary doghouse complete with an annoyingly persistent barking dog, all topped off with a stone shithouse. Nice.

Not much of a square, anymore.

Dean cleared his voice and Trev finished with the local foursome. "At ease."

Chastised, they stood, open legs and arms folded behind their backs.

Dean smiled. "Sorry to beat you men up but this comes with instructing. Don't take it personally. Put on a brave face."

They didn't smile back.

"This parade square looks like an obstacle course. Does it serve any other purpose?"

Walt piped up, "Citizen Lionel comes here to praise our Lord twice a day, sir!"

"Ah. So, we can clean this area up and it's okay with you?" asked Dean.

"Yes sir."

"Let's do an inspection of these soldiers first. Carry on with the practice, men. Start basic. Go around the perimeter of this square as best you can."

Trev complied, dashing to the crowd of troops milling around. He barked, "Fall in! Line up and count off!"

Dean watched as Dan, Rick and Trev scurried off with the local angel trio following. The parade square was full of mystified people milling around, dressed in army fatigues and hats. More Farmers Market than polished military.

This could take a while.

Dean turned about face and went to see a woman about a horse.

TERRY AND JESS painstakingly trudged along picking up rocks and throwing them on the stone boat while the horses watched in mild bemusement.

"Are the horses laughing at us?" said Jess.

"They aren't saying if they are."

"Are you sure that was Dean in the army truck?" Jess lifted a respectably round boulder and tossed it on the boat which hit with a satisfying clank.

Terry shook her head. "No. I couldn't get a very good look because a couple of horses who shall remain nameless were jumping around being a pain in the ass!"

The horses looked back at her.

"Yes, probably laughing at us."

"Look Aunty. An army guy is headed our way."

"I see that. Keep working. Maybe he's nosy or wants a date."

"That'd be cool!"

"It'd be me, kiddo. You young 'uns aren't allowed any friskiness around here."

Terry kept him in the corner of her eye as he slowly got closer. He was having a good look around as he headed their way. Nosy?

Then he vanished from her view.

"Where did he go?" asked Jess.

"The cans, maybe? Along the rock fence checking the defenses we're building?"

"It could be he wasn't coming here after all. Hobnobbing with the bosses of this place."

They both leaned down to the business of rock picking and sweating it out in the field.

"Did you miss me?" Came a voice from the other side of the horses.

Terry went around the other side and spotted the soldier grinning like a fool. She rushed him and they clutched each other hard for five minutes.

"Oh, hey Dean. Let me take the reins so the horses don't run off," Jess offered.

The pair said nothing. Finally the embrace unclenched enough for Terry to ask a few questions. "What are you doing way the hell up here?"

"I'm a captain training this National Guard unit. And you?"

"I'm 'Gina' and over there is 'Greta' who's looking for her father."

Dean added, "...and you found what seems to be some Disciples show in progress?"

"Yes, some weirdness happening."

"Let's walk and talk. Bring Jess...I mean Greta and your team. We need this rock pile you have in that sled. Drag it down to the parade square."

They all looked at the scene of a hundred or so citizen soldiers stumbling around aimlessly on the square with officers shouting at them, making it worse.

Terry shook her head. "It looks like ten little kid's soccer teams turned loose at the same time, in the same uniform."

"It does. I'm hoping these rocks will be a perimeter guide to their route and reduce the confusion."

Jess led the horses while Terry and Dean walked together but far enough apart not to raise suspicions. The horses gently pulled the awful stone boat along behind, runners occasionally screeching the hulking sled over rocks in the driveway.

"Dean, why are you here?"

"David Bradley sent Trev and I up here as airstrip runway workers by day and army instructors a few nights a week. The General President...'Brant'? called him and said some peculiar things are happening."

"General Brant! I met him when I found the Ukraine A-bombs and missing astronauts last year. Nice guy."

"Oh my god..." muttered Dean, shaking his head. "You know him?"

"You should phone me more often."

Dean protested, "I did! I called your office in Ottawa. They said you didn't work there, which is rubbish, isn't it?"

"That's because I went to England, did some work for Sandros Hammar and then quit the RCMP right afterwards. Jess and I have a mansion in London. You should visit."

"Geez. Oh yes, Joyce is setting up the FBI office in town."

"Wow." Terry leaned over to him. "Don't take this as an insult Captain but that is the saddest bunch of marching soldiers, I've ever seen. A mother duck and her ducklings being chased by a fox could do a better job. We have sheep that could do better—"

"Thanks, I get your point!"

"So, we have a load of rocks. What's your plan?" asked Jess.

"Park the stone boat right here and let's get some manpower."

---

TREV SCANNED the troops wandering the square in dribbles and clumps, flailing their arms in general confusion like chickens in a coop. The big square was a ragged circle of camouflaged, bewildered humanity. The angels didn't help with their shouting and threatening. He wondered for an instant if his old job at Royal security was still available.

"Lieutenant... Trev! Over here!" Dean called, waving at him.

Trev arrived out of breath. He smiled at Terry and Jess. "What the hell are you two doing here?"

"Long story. We'll get together later," whispered Terry.

"Trev, get those guys over here to pick up a handful of rocks. Lay them out along the edges in a big square. Put a few in a smaller square in the middle." Dean pointed for directions.

"A visual guide?"

"Yes. Let's try this."

Trev shouted, "Halt!"

Two hundred bewildered feet stumbled to a stop.

"Eyes left!"

One hundred and ninety-nine eyes turned left including the soldier with a black eye patch.

"Here on the double!"

Two hundred annoyed legs stopped, then hustled to the stone boat. They formed up in two lines.

"Pick up a rock! Place them in a square on the perimeter!"

Two hundred willing hands cleaned off every rock and rushed out to lay them down in the guiding rows as Rick and Dan demonstrated. They were back in five minutes.

"We need more rocks Dean," mumbled Trev.

Terry turned the horses towards the field she and Jess worked. "Follow me, men! We have lots more rocks in the field for you.

Trev shouted, "Form up triple file."

They scrambled around to make three lines.

Dan called to them. "Left foot thirty inches per step, heel first, right arm with your left leg, twenty-inch swing."

Trev called, "Forward march."

The long line of men clumped behind Terry and her two horses pulling the stone boat to the rocky field. Two big mangy hounds came along to chase and bark at their owners as they trudged along the rough roadway.

"Go home Rufus!" hissed one man as the dog yanked on his pant leg.

Rufus the dog went from joyous to crushed feelings in one phrase. He stopped, turned and slunk away.

Trev leaned to Dean. "They aren't doing a bad job marching this time. Not... terrible, anyway."

Dean shook his head and mumbled to himself, "Terry Reid, the weirdest Pied Piper in Alaska."

---

JESS WALKED beside Terry and the horses as they led the procession of soldiers marching the half mile up to the stone field they worked on. She heard the horses clip-clopping along and puffing occasionally, snorting with Terry giving some instructions while two hundred fumbling army boots stomped along behind them.

Terry seemed to be enjoying this simple life in the backwoods of the continent. It was like she hadn't a care in the world.

Jess glanced at the mass of men, heads lowered, trudging along, sweating, looking bored and unhappy. They were trying to keep in time with each other, occasionally bumping into the soldier in front. Marching to oblivion.

Suddenly Terry broke into a loud song.

"Ain't no use in lookin' down!" Terry sang loudly with not a bad singing voice.

A few men echoed back, "Ain't no discharge on the ground ..."

Terry replied, "Ain't no use in lookin' back."

The echo was, "Jody's got your Cadillac ..."

"Ain't no use in lookin' blue."

"Jody's got your girlfriend, too."

"Sound off."

And they seemed to know what to do from there.

The officers immediately picked up the song, singing loud and proud while a few of the men sang along. It took three repetitions before everyone chimed in quite well and suddenly marched to the beat. Their heads perked up and the shoulders went back proudly stepping towards a field to get a pocketful of rocks.

There were sweet and powerful voices intermingled with the men. Jess thought a few of them must have been professional singers in their previous lives. They were clearly excellent to lead the other voices.

Kids ran along beside them in the dirt and grass singing along with their dads, brothers and uncles. She was glad Terry selected a song version not having bad words in it. Jess found herself singing along too, barely shaking her head.

Walking and singing with horses leading the troops in a northern Disciples cult. Typical Terry adventure.

JOYCE GOT into the sheriff's office Sunday morning courtesy of Rick's key and his security pass code. He'd told her as much as he knew about Samuel's terrible death.

Clutching her heavy briefcase, she walked into the office and called out, "Anyone here? FBI!"

Dead silent.

Saying 'FBI' never got old. Once she snuck it into the conversation at an excruciatingly boring blind date. He blathered on about how important he was to a local software company and was usually too over scheduled to date anyone. Joyce 'should feel lucky' he said. Disgusted, she pulled out her credentials and said 'FBI' and... poof... he was gone.

Jerk. Everyone has a guilty conscience. You just have to spark it up.

AFTER THE TROOPS LEFT, Jess kept up their lonely job of picking rocks from the field while Terry herded the nearby horses.

"Not many rocks left, kid," her aunty smiled.

"It's picked over by the troops... no pun intended."

Jess noticed Terry wistfully watching the soldiers singing and marching around the newly lined square. "Those rocks made the difference for those dirt rangers. They can find their way."

"Dirt Rangers?"

"A nick name the Americans call anyone who's trying to be a soldier with a long way to go."

"Ah."

Terry narrowed her eyes. "Looks like one of the officers has hopped in that truck and is coming this way."

"Not Trev or Dean?"

"No. Keep working."

They kept picking the rocks up and throwing them into the stone boat though they had to move around the field to get the stragglers after the troops cleaned off the easiest ones. Slim pickens. The army truck pulled up to the highest point in their field and stopped.

Jess looked over at it. "Getting out…closing the door…opening the back…looks like a big drone thing…"

"Thanks for the narration, Miss Writer. I can see that."

"Cool! The drone is flying and going around the camp. Now it's following the troops in the square. Jetsons looking over MASH."

"Get picking."

Jess glumly went back to picking. It seemed other people were marching, watching, flying drones while she did this drudgery.

Out of the corner of her eye she saw the drone return to the truck. "Hey, he's done. Put it away. He's coming this way."

The dirty green truck stopped about thirty feet from them. A large man, one of the Lieutenants that came with Dean, got out and headed their way.

"I wonder what he wants?"

"Just play dumb Marlene Dietrich."

"No, my name is Greta! You're Gina!"

"Oh, yeah, right."

Terry and Jess threw a last rock on the sled and stood up.

The man arrived and called, "Hi folks. Thought I'd stop by and tell you what I'm doing. I parked back there so I wouldn't spook the horses. I'm a vet in real life. …and the town coroner."

*Probably one of the diggers in the rain when I got here. He was the leader.*

"You're a busy guy," said Terry, poker faced.

"My name is Dr. Richard Forest. Call me Rick."

He shook hands with them. Jess held back a grin when she said 'Greta' and noticed Terry managed a straight faced 'Gina'.

Rick was a big, solid man, late forties, with big strong hands. He had a large friendly, craggy face. There was a military manner to him, deeply ingrained and not just a recent National Guard thing. He'd been around the world block a few times.

"You were probably wondering what I was up to. I used my drone to do a camera scan of the camp and the soldiers for Washington. They like to evaluate what we are doing and make sure we aren't sleeping on the job."

Terry added, "Slick machine and a fair size drone."

"It is. I have quite a large one I use in my real vet job for farmers and ranchers to look around their spreads to see who's been eating their critters. I have a little weapons pack I use if they want to knock them off, too."

Jess added, "Like drones in the middle east?"

Rick looked at her and smiled. "Not quite. These are Hammar rotary versions so they are more manoeuvrable and can carry more."

"Ah. 'Hammar' tech. Heard of him."

"My machines are big enough to carry calves or a colt under it with a sling."

He looked at Terry, "Thanks for adding the cadence songs for us. It made a huge difference."

"Sure."

"You seem to know a bit about the military."

She barely shrugged. "Saw some marching stuff on TV."

Jess added, "The community guard don't carry guns when they're marching. That's unusual for an army parade, isn't it?"

Rick looked back at the soldiers, singing and marching now seeming like it was their favourite thing ever. "They only have 'rubbers', anyway. No point."

Terry perked up, "Only rubber guns?"

"Yes. If they have the real deal we haven't seen them."

"Marching for looks?"

"Could be. This place doesn't want their Guardsman armed. Not sure what they're cooking up here but it's not good."

Terry and Jess shook their heads in agreement.

He winked and walked away. Jess and Terry watched him drive back to the parade square.

"Holy shit, Aunty. Does he know who we really are?"

"Word is getting around, alright. We need to find your dad and get out of here very soon."

———

RICK STARTED up the truck and it slowly rambled down to the marching square. It had been an interesting day. They'd turned a bunch of sullen marooned labourers into a decent bunch of marchers with a song from a female horse driver.

That driver didn't look like a cult community dweller. They tended to look fearful, beat down and locked up with no place to go but she didn't seem to fear anything or anyone.

He needed to look into this tonight.

Dean, Trev and Dan were already walking towards him when he drove up. Dismissed troops were wandering off in all directions, greeted by enthusiastic friends and family. Everyone loves a parade.

"Got some publicity shots for us?" asked Dan.

"I did. Swept around the place and surroundings while I was at it. We could put it on a tourist brochure if we wanted. A picturesque northern gulag."

Dan smirked. "I can see the motto: 'sign your life away and work like a dog.'"

The four hopped in and Rick slowly drove the truck out through the gates. He leaned out and waved at Terry and Jess picking rocks in the sun.

"Were you talking to them?" asked Dan seated to his right.

"Yes."

"The usual rock pickers getting broken in?"

"I don't think that's the usual pair at all."

Rick nodded and in the rear mirror saw Trev and Dean casually look at each other at their mention. One of them might have winked but he couldn't be sure.

# 14

## AN OLD HAUNT

Joyce tiptoed around the sheriff's office with the usual sense of dread. She wondered if the rough handling she and her partner Anna suffered in Washington didn't give her flashbacks.

*Pull on your big girl pants and move on!*

She didn't turn on any lights as she worked her way into the rear of the building's main floor. There was plenty of Alaska daylight to see where she was going. At last, she came to the FBI office door and called out, "Hello?"

Using the key Rick gave her she opened the door and peeked in. She made her way around the corridor looking for her office. Here it was!

Rick's grim homemade morgue table greeted her.

She closed the door behind her, plopped her briefcase on the floor near the impromptu slab and opened it. She dug out the short and nasty pry bar Rick loaned her and kicked the briefcase to one side. She stabbed the edge of the pry bar under the plywood edge fiercely and pushed down on the bar as hard as she could. The cheap nails screeched as they lost their grip. The edge popped up. She went over to the other side and stabbed the bar under the edge and leaned into it, hard. It also screamed and groaned until it lost its purchase. The disgusting stained slab popped off the desks like a side of fried bacon.

She now had two desks for her office.

Joyce leaned the plywood slab on edge and pushed it to the wall with her foot. One desk went to the rear of the room and the other went to the front. She would hunt up a few chairs on her way back from the washroom. The coffee was beginning to back up in all the excitement.

She found the washroom and hesitated. *Men's*

She remembered what Sally, the receptionist said, went inside, chose a stall, and securely locked it. Just in time.

The bathroom door squeaked open and thumped closed. She saw official looking men shoes going by, under the door. The boots paused at the end stall, went in and slammed the door. A belt-buckle jingled, pants and a gun belt hit the floor. There was a pause, grunt, splash and a fart and then someone started whistling.

This was awkward. She sat quietly, waiting him out.

After five minutes, which seemed like an hour, she heard the paper roller going, a flush and pants going back up and a belt-buckle jingle. She spotted the boots going to the sink and there were sounds of someone vigorously washing their hands then drying them. The boots squeaked towards the door then paused.

Whack!

The person in the boots slapped her stall door so hard it was all she could do to keep from screaming. She jumped off the seat and mumbled in a weak voice. "F...F...BI!"

The man in the boots laughed for what seemed hours. He finally stopped and said, "I'm Sheriff Abe, Miss FBI. I'll have some coffee ready when you're done so wash your hands.

How humiliating!

JOYCE FOUND her way into the break room and spotted the grinning sheriff. Taking a breath, she joined him and dug out a coffee mug after making sure it was clean. It said, 'Kissed a Sheriff Lately?'

The sheriff poured her coffee as he said, "Joyce Carson? You're the new FBI agent up here?"

"I am. And you are the sheriff."

"Correct."

No handshake. Sheriff Abe saw she was five seven, stocky, looked like she worked out, serious and intense. He'd best see what her record was.

"What became of my predecessor?"

"Samuel's deceased. A long time ago he decided he was needing a change and ran off to join one of those communities. The coroner decided to look for him and dug him out of a sheep field."

"...and?"

"He was old, a bit of a drunk and was dead. What can I say?"

"As far as you are concerned 'case closed'?"

"That is correct."

---

WAS this guy part of the conspiracy, up for re-election and needed the votes, or just lazy?

Joyce took a sip of coffee which was very good. She had him figured at about five foot eleven, thin, about mid-thirties, unmarried, didn't look like he worked out much, hunched, a bit sloppy of dress so not an ex-military man. He had a few tats and scars. She'd look him up when she got to her computer.

The sheriff continued, "I see you found your office. Rick's home-made morgue slab is in there."

"I did. Mr. Forest loaned me a pry bar to get access to the desks. You wouldn't happen to know where the FBI car went?"

"I do. It's a Jeep at the back of the vehicle compound. You might have to jump start it. It hasn't run for months. Keys are at the front desk."

"Are the department files still here?" she asked.

"They are in the drawers in the office. I think they're locked up and we don't have keys for it. They might smell of blood and formaldehyde though."

"There should be a laptop with this office, too," she added.

"Right. It's at the front desk. The receptionist used it while we were waiting for Samuel to return. I'm sure he wouldn't mind."

"Thank you, Sheriff."

Joyce left him and went to her office and tried Rick's keys. They worked! She opened the file cabinets and glanced into their contents. There were some interesting files which she would go through later.

Leaving her coffee, she strode down the hall to the reception area and spotted a lap top computer with a huge label, 'FBI', on the top. She unplugged the power cord, scooped up the machine and returned to her office. *I wonder if it works?*

The passwords for the router and computer were written nicely on a sticker on the front, just before the keyboard, with an accompanying message. *Steal me and access all these important files with these passwords and they buy me a better one. You're welcome Mr. Burglar.*

She plugged it in and was confronted with a screen saver of the receptionist and her latest boyfriend wielding AR military type rifles while they wore cowboy hats.

A hillbilly yee-ha! Joyce ripped off the old sticker and replaced it with the official logo of the FBI, the owner of the computer. Foreboding and imperious.

*Beware, evil-doers!*

---

DES FOUND himself humming as he walked along with his horses pulling the stone boat. The birds sang nearby as Gina and Greta busily picked rocks of all shapes and sizes from the ploughed field and threw them on the sled. The sun warmed his back in the early morning.

He saw kids going into the little school while their parents went off to do the various chores in their village. It had taken months, but he had to admit his life had turned for the better and it seemed so did many of the inhabitants.

"You look deep in thought Des," asked the young girl, Greta.

Smart, sharp and hard working, this one.

"Yes. I was thinking this isn't such a bad place, other than the bosses which is the same anywhere else."

"Are you changing your mind?"

"I am. Have you watched parents with children in the city? Parents are rushing to make money and the kids are pushed along like nuisances. There's no joy in it for any of them."

"As a kid myself, I like to think we're a treasure." She winked and tossed a couple medium boulders on the sled.

"I agree. Parents are pushing the timecard with their children while staring at their cell phones, telling other parents how kids spend too much time on their electronic toys."

"You're saying turn off the gadgets and enjoy your kids?"

"I am and this is the place to do it."

---

JOYCE DRILLED down into file manager and had a look at what was important enough to be kept. The file names were fairly non-descript. Was there a clue in here about what Samuel was looking for? How about an easy "In case I go missing—arrest this guy".

Nothing obvious.

Lionel warranted quite a big file. She dug around in it and saw some names such as Isaac and Jeb, currently labeled as Angels. What was that? As she drilled down into the file they mentioned 'Lionel Garson' aka George M. Valentine, was a push for 53674 Corp. He was listed for petty larceny and money laundering in his younger days.

The Enforcer Angels had lurid records in LA for assault and battery with jail time. Tommy Giordano and Alexi Gormakov picked up the religious names 'Jeb' and Isaac' for community authenticity and credibility. An unsavoury bunch in robes.

She couldn't find a record of an Abe Kelly anywhere. He didn't exist. Her gaze drifted in the direction of his office. Strange.

Back to the computer.

Richard Forest was there as a lifetime resident of Alaska who'd put in his time in Special Forces in Iraq, returned to a veterinarian practice and had a number of sensational divorces. Wife number four jumped off a cliff into the Alaska River and her body was never found.

Ex-agent Samuel was from Washington state but had been a comrade of Rick's in their Army days in Iraq. He had his demons judging from the odd spell of "LOA – personal reasons". His book-keeping was sketchy and poorly kept up.

Hot on the trail or pickled?

Joyce leaned back and wondered what she had in this office. Seemed local skeletons were in every closet in every home while a number of folks were walking around using aliases. She looked at the time. Eleven o'clock. She'd go see if the Jeep would start and then grab a sandwich. She might have to kiss up to the sheriff for a jump start.

She locked her files and office door, collected the vehicle keys and stepped into the compound. There it was—a very dirty four door Jeep station wagon.

Next to the jeep was a big trailer with *Forest–Survey Drone Service* printed on the side. The drone must be huge. *Hammar Tech* was also emblazoned on the sides. He must keep it here because it's safer in a police compound than a vet's yard. Expensive.

She went back to snooping around the disheveled jeep. Her walk around told her the tires were good, lights weren't broken, and it had no bullet holes.

No police paint job for this machine. Incognito-ish. It had a faded black complexion. A ghost car owned by a dead guy. Nice.

She popped the hood and saw there was oil in the engine and there wasn't a cat or nest of pack rats on the air filter. It had a big V8, all the hidden lights and sirens with dual batteries and the other cop car specialty stuff. No dip sticks for the automatic transmission so it must be a manual. A manly machine.

Little whistle gismos were placed on the roof, one on each side catching her eye. Plastic warning horn for some purpose?

Must be a country thing.

A crack of thunder made her jump. She looked up to see the menacing clouds piling up and the rain started to hammer down.

She pulled the door open. The hinges creaked. The stink of old food and dead air greeted her. She shrugged and climbed into the hot vehicle which had been cooking in the sun for months. The heat, rain and humidity made the vehicle choking.

Samuel wasn't much for cleaning his vehicle out. She'd ask Abe about where the shotgun and tear gas went. It took her twenty minutes to scoop out the fastfood debris, old clothes and gumbo mud caked on the floors. It had current vehicle ID and insurance in case Abe decided to bust her for vehicular violations.

Digging through the clothing pockets unearthed nothing. There were a number of gas station receipts scattered on the floor, all from "Floyds Gas and Service". She looked up the address and saw Floyds was the last gas station on the pavement before hitting the gravel to drive into the communities. The receipts went in her pocket for later.

Was that the only place he went? Why? Should I get this car finger-printed? She doubted Abe was interested. When the cops aren't interested, who do you call? The town vet?

She stuck in the key and gave it a turn. Reluctantly it growled and cranked the engine over for ten seconds and barely started. Yay for dual batteries. It obviously needed a run. She put it in gear and headed for Floyds Gas.

She turned up the radio and hummed along to a local rock station. The wipers went with the beat as they barely kept up to the hard rain. Joyce had to admit she was enjoying the stick shift and big engine. This thing was fast for an SUV wagon. Cop specs. All it needed was a sweep out and wash and it would be fabulous.

She made the drive to Floyd's at noon. The rainstorm stopped as abruptly as it started. The gas tank was alarmingly low, so she pulled up to the pump and stood while Floyd himself offered graciously to top it up. While the pump ran, he checked under the hood and cleaned the windshield.

"So, you're the FBI lady," Floyd asked with a smile.

"Agent Joyce. Is it Floyd or Mr. Floyd?"

"Floyd's fine. That's the only name people use around here."

"Good to meet you, Floyd."

They stood and listened as the ancient gas pump wheezed fuel into her Jeep.

"Do you recognize this vehicle, Floyd?"

"Sure do. Samuel came here lots of times with it."

"Ah."

The gas pump grumbled away, slowly pumping life into the jeep.

"Where do you suppose Samuel was going, burning all this gas? Seems odd, doesn't it?"

"Not really. He had a girl friend out at the East community. I think he settled out there... a herder I believe."

"Ah. Is your café open?"

"It is. If you want, you can get some chow and I'll add the gas on the bill."

"Sure. Let me move it to the side."

After moving the jeep, Joyce stepped into the run down double-wide trailer that served as Floyd's Café. It looked clean despite its age. There were a dozen tables and three dozen chairs, mismatched but functional. A coffee shop on a budget.

"What would y'all like today?" an older lady asked with a strong southern accent. She looked Joyce, over stopping her eyes on the uniforms' FBI badge.

"Menu, please."

Joyce watched the staff over the top of the menu noticing the other two waitresses, quite young, wore proper dresses dating back to the 1990's.

"I'll have the soup and a coffee."

"Large?"

"Sure."

"Sourdough bread with it?"

"Why not?"

The young waitress rushed over to pour her coffee and scoop the menu, all the while being watched by the older lady. Floyd came in and handed her the gas bill and a few instructions.

A pecking order.

A giant bowl of soup and a slab of bread arrived. It looked delicious. She barely managed to eat it all.

"Got room for strawberry apple pie? Just out of the oven."

"I'll take a piece to go. I'll pay up, too."

The older lady figured out the bill by hand with a pencil on a simple handbill. "Lunch with gas $56.49."

Joyce pulled a charge card out of her pocket. "I'm washing dishes if you don't take credit cards," she joked.

The lady didn't crack a smile but dug out an elderly credit card machine. She laboriously placed the card on the machine, then the carbon paper receipt, held it down with her left hand while stroking the mechanical slider back and forth with her right. Joyce was impressed at this museum quality demonstration.

"And here's your receipt."

"Don't you get the internet out here?"

The lady looked at Joyce seriously. "The internet is evil and electronic cards are the mark of the devil."

"Ah, of course it is."

The lady said nothing.

"By the way, where is the East Community located?"

The lady nervously looked at Joyce's FBI badge and uniform, again. "I don't drive. Ask Floyd."

"Do you live there?"

"I'll give you directions, Agent Joyce," Floyd interrupted while the lady and her young charges retreated. "I have a map over here."

*Struck a nerve?*

"Are you connected with the communities, Floyd?"

He played the genial 'awe-shucks old guy' card. "You could say we help around this place on their behalf."

"I see."

"Here's the map to get to the East Community. Go right, pick up the 73 road which is the first gravel road on your right out of here, then travel about forty miles and you'll come to the big stone gate. Best give them a call before you arrive."

*Perhaps I should ...next time! The FBI doesn't need to call ahead!*

"...and the last ten miles will be drying from this rain. It'll be gumbo for a few hours."

*What's gumbo?*

"Thanks Floyd. I won't be going out there just yet. It's getting late," she lied.

Joyce pulled out of the gas station and tipped her left turn signal. She waited for a tractor trailer carrying a load of logs to come by. On impulse, she turned the jeep right instead, headed to the 73 road, first road on her right and made a big rooster trail of muck behind her on the narrow gravel road.

She didn't know Floyd watched her leave and had already phoned the East Community to warn Lionel the FBI was coming.

Joyce found the gravel road narrow but mostly smooth. The wet gravel splattered all over her vehicle covering the windows. She turned on her wipers, pushing the window sprayer occasionally to keep them clear. This must be why Floyd said skip the drive today. Too late now.

The wet small hills had washboards which rattled her and the vehicle until she learned to ease off on the gas. There were a few homes along the way, mostly with farms and ranches. They didn't look very prosperous.

She saw a sign that simply said 'East – 10 Miles'. The road narrowed and the gravel vanished. The surface looked smooth and pristine. Her jeep drove like it was in ice as soon as it hit it. The road was too narrow to go back now.

She felt the tires clogging up with great lumps of sticky mud throwing them to the side and on top of the hood. The less she pressed the gas the better her traction seemed to be. The traction control cut in and out to drive all the wheels, sometimes a help and other times a nuisance. The road surface was a cross between jello and the stickiest peanut butter.

*Ah, legendary gumbo!* Now she understood.

The Jeep squished along the mud churning it up behind her. Eventually she went through a thickly wooded section of forest, crossed the river and appeared above the community adjacent to a field. There were three workers throwing rocks onto a sled. That must be Terry and Jess. Dean said they were on rock patrol.

Joyce did a careful U turn in a grassy section, rolled down a window and waved out to the rock pickers.

"Directions…lost," she called to them.

She could see Terry marching towards her while the others kept working.

"Good to see you Terry. Dean and Trev told me all about it."

"Hey Joyce! Welcome to nowhere! I see you've discovered gumbo."

"I have. Strange stuff."

Terry lifted a foot up with four inches of grey gumbo firmly glued on to it. "It's a clay. They make crude pots and sculptures with it up here."

"Charming."

Terry glanced around. "We'd best speed this up. An angel will be tracking up the gumbo to chase off the intruders."

"Your angels are just a trio of scumbag low-lifes from the city, but you already knew that."

"Yes. This crowd is planning something involving a National Guard group, unarmed, and something to do with getting mineral rights to homestead sections. Everyone here is hiding from something."

Joyce looked in her rear-view mirror and nodded. "I see an angel is working his way up here now. Floyd must have called and warned them. Any trouble from them?"

Terry smiled. "Not much, yet."

"I see."

"I suspect Samuel was onto their plan and paid the price."

"I saw the cops digging him out of a sheep field a few weeks ago. Watch your back. Be careful who you trust."

"By the way, my name is Gina and Jess is Greta."

Joyce shook her head. "Of course, it is."

"Here comes our guardian angel, emphasis on the guard part."

Jeb came puffing up to the Jeep, trying to scruff off the gumbo coating his boots. The fellow looked angry but pasted on a smile when he saw Joyce's FBI shoulder patch. "Hello…er…Agent…"

Not attempting to brave the mud she stayed safe in the vehicle and flashed him her credentials. "Agent Joyce. And you are?"

Jeb dodged her question and turned to Terry, "Back to work. I got this!"

She winked at him and left.

Joyce tried to keep him on track. "Sorry to interfere with work but I'm lost. Can I get back to the highway through here… Mr…"

"Jeb, call me Jeb."

"Sure Jeb. Can I get through here?"

"No, this is the end of the road so go back the way you came."

There was an awkward silence, but his aggression seethed.

"Follow your tracks."

"I will do that Jeb. Have a fine day."

He stepped back as Joyce gently pulled away, slipping and sliding. Jeb reminded her of the jerks at the old sheriff's office in her previous life. It was all she could do to not give him the finger as she drove away.

Mr. Congeniality.

She was back in town in forty-five minutes, ran the Jeep through the car wash then headed home for a shower. Living at the No Tell Motel was getting tiring. It didn't seem like a long-term living space.

---

JOYCE, Dean and Trev got together for dinner at Yukon Fatties selecting a secluded booth in the far back, away from prying ears. They were soon swapping stories, new and old.

Dean mumbled while eating a cheese omelette, "Couldn't believe it when I saw Terry and Jess at this cult farm in Alaska. Says she lives in London now."

Trev added, "I lost track of Terry when she left DC. It's not like we call home each week."

"You two know there's a function on your phone to look shit up, right?"

Trev and Dean nodded like they knew.

"You don't know, do you?"

They both paused, stopped chewing, and shrugged.

Joyce looked down at her phone and typed in 'Theresa Reid – wiki'. A line of text appeared. "Listen up you two.

"*Major Theresa Margaret Reid – Adventurer ...born May 14, 2001 in Prince Rupert, BC, Canada... notorious Mountie and Army Special Forces... informant in Montreal and Vancouver, responsible for thirty-two convictions of the mob family and biker organizations... four years in Afghanistan Army intelligence gathering ... escaped the final destruction of all UN forces and facilities. ...sent to the US in 2030 where she is rumoured to have solved the notorious Disciples fires and murders climaxing in the famous Revisionist Convention shoot out ...personally arrested William Page.*

Trev and Dean looked at each other and Dean said, "We know that. We were there, too. No rumour about it."

She shrugged and continued reading, "*Reid is said to have hunted down a rogue Russian faction planting a series of mysterious 'Verbeelding-face-viewers' causing a number of deaths. In 2031 she found the kidnapped President Casio which ended in his unexplained death and turmoil ... (redacted)...she caused the banning of the CIA which triggered a military takeover of the U.S. ...(redacted)... Her story has been recently challenged by U.S. officials...(redacted)...US military now claiming credit for solving Revisionist bombings and election tampering. Reid has left the country... *"

"Sounds like Terry, alright," said Dean, impressed.

Joyce said, "there's more. *Addition: Major Reid transferred to London, England where she rescued six astronauts and captured two lost US atomic bombs which the Americans reclaimed. (redacted) She subsequently resigned from the RCMP becoming a 'for hire' private investigator working the cases (redacted) and (redacted).*

*"As far as is known she lives in a private estate somewhere in London, England."*

Trev grinned, "That's our Terry! Infamous while being mysterious."

"And officially redacted information on Wikipedia! The long arm of somebody who's very touchy."

Joyce snorted. *"Hollywood page: The movie based on Major Theresa Reid called 'Viewers of Death' was a flop. WWE star Grant 'Block of Granite' Stone was the American Green Beret called 'Reid' who singlehandedly saves America from Communist Russians wearing killer face viewers but not from his own awful acting. Biggest movie bomb in modern memory."*

"Another expensive Hollywood history lesson down the drain," said Dean, draining the last of his coffee.

"Can you follow me over to the sheriff's office? I have that Army van to drop off. I now have a jeep."

"Sure. Your FBI Jeep looks decent. Big wash and clean out?"

"Yes. I found some odd receipts and a lot of food wrappers, clumps of mud and newspapers."

Dean picked up the bill and scootched across the vinyl on the booth. "We gotta go. National Guard meeting, tonight."

---

In London Richard got a call from a special number on his mobile phone. With trepidation he answered. "Yes m...Mr. Hobson?"

A terse voice spoke. "Have you located Terry Reid yet?"

"Um, not yet sir."

"Why not? What have you been doing?"

"I've been busy."

"Spending my money and doing nothing?"

"Hey, it wasn't easy getting close to the Reids. I don't just phone them. She's all over the world! Amelia Pun is the connection to them and their mansion."

"Just break in. I thought you were some kind of a spy."

"I researched their mansion carefully and it's a high-tech job from Sandros Hammer himself. He has guard clones in there. The only way in is through the girl."

"When?"

"I'll put on some pressure over the next couple of days. She—or her phone must contain the details."

"Twenty-four hours!"

The phone went dead.

# 15

# A ROOM WITH A VIEW

Joyce parked her jeep in front of the small apartment building and tapped on the landlord's door. She heard noise behind the door and waited. She looked around the front of the Belvedere Apartments and was mildly impressed. It had received a coat of paint recently and the grass looked to have been mowed within the past week. Not bad.

The door opened and an old face greeted her.

Joyce assumed her poker face. "FBI. You the owner of this building?"

"Yup."

"And you are?"

"Grady."

"Did Samuel Bemon live here, Grady?"

"Yup."

"Could you show me his apartment?"

"Sure, but it's empty. He ain't paid rent for months. Wanna rent it?"

"I want to see it if it hasn't been disturbed."

They clumped down the wooden boardwalk serving as a sidewalk until they came to vacated room seven. It looked like Grady's pickup was backed into the door area to clear out Samuel's furnishings.

He opened the door and waved her in. "After you."

Joyce flicked the light on and glanced around the room. "Grubby."

"Yeah, well, I just emptied the room and haven't cleaned it yet."

Joyce looked at him, waiting for more words. When none came, she pointed to the old Chevy at the door. "Is that his stuff in this pickup?"

"Yup."

"Where are you dumping it?"

"The dump."

"When?"

"A day or two."

"Give me an hour to sift through it?"

"Sure. Might be some good stuff in there."

At first, she perished the thought of reusing the stuff but thought she'd look at it first.

She scanned the room. Decent place. Had a small stove, kitchen table, chairs and a fridge. "How much is the rent?"

"Three hundred bucks a month, just like this, plus utilities."

She pulled out her traveling cash and peeled off the necessary bills. "I'll take it, but I get fifty bucks off if I clean it myself." *I'll check for evidence and I'm cheap.*

"Deal!" he said, grinning as he stuffed the cash away. "I'll come for the pick-up in a couple of hours. Go for it."

Joyce shifted the used mattress aside to salvage a small dresser and a bed spring from the pick-up. A girl has to draw the line, somewhere.

Surely David Bradley wouldn't leave her here forever... would he?

She decided the landlord was itchy to take his truck, so she lugged the rest of Samuels' stuff back into the room, moving it all to where it likely resided. It looked much better in the room than in the truck, headed for the dump. Besides, maybe it held a clue or two about his demise.

It was time to triage this treasure trove.

The mattress did look to be brand new and under plastic. She could cover it with a couple of sheets, so it would be fine for the length of time of her stay in Maclean. Shifting the mattress again, it flipped, revealing a pocket sewn on its underside. She could see something hard and lumpy was jammed inside. After some tugging, she had a bent up three ring binder that appeared to have been through the wars. She carefully opened it and perused the handwritten pages then closed it again. For study, later.

As she pawed through the rest of Samuel's belongings, she noticed how oddly impersonal they all were. He had to have been living somewhere else and showed up, did laundry and then left again. No food or way to prepare food. There was little evidence of him eating at home.

Other than Samuel's clothes, she had all the furniture back in the room approximately where they were, judging by the dust bunnies. Next step was to clean the place up. She made a quick trip to the local store for cleaning supplies, some canned food, bread, tea and milk and a secondhand vacuum and some new bedding.

The used vacuum cleaner was a bit of a bust. It made a lot of noise and had very little pucker but did help somewhat. A bit of elbow grease and Samuel's old place looked and smelled fresher. The new bedding was cheap but clean, wasn't fancy, but it did the job.

Home sweet home.

Time to go back and check out of her hotel room. She stole a few hotel towels to take with her. Nobody's going to report the FBI.

In her new abode she made herself a cup of tea from the room kettle and settled down to read the binder she'd found. Entries were hand-written from his first day which explained why the computer was hardly used. A paper copy may have served as his security system as did his awful hand-writing.

Entries were vague. They started three years before she got there. She'd have to cross index for actual dates as many were ongoing and spanned years. They didn't follow official code.

There were a few that stuck out for Joyce.

Case #309: HO (Head office?) called and told me to go to the Russian border and watch for thirty-six hours to see if illegal crossings were happening. After freezing my ass off I saw thirty-six people of all ages and sizes going back and forth, all local indigenous inhabitants or dressed in that fashion. Infiltration was possible with local knowledge and transportation. Duly reported back and received no feedback.

Case #309A: Fourteen days later HO said go back and spot check for incidents of smuggling. Went back and spot checked finding normal furs, pelts, cell phones, personal hunting weapons and food stuffs. Met an extremely short man with a beard carrying an accordion who didn't speak. The others seemed embarrassed about him and appeared to shun him. Reported this to HO and received no reply.

Case#602: HO ordered ongoing surveillance of the four local Motion communities. Talked to some inhabitants about town. Found them friendly but vague. Name/rank/serial number. Many claimed to be well versed musicians. Mostly arty-evangelical-philosophers with few scientist types unless homeopaths or naturopaths count. Inhabitants seemed like squirrels hoarding for the end of the world. Their doom dates occasionally come and go.

Case#856: HO wanted more information about life in the camp. The IRS is convinced they were not getting their due. Will attempt to go under cover at the East Community.

Case#856A: Showed up and told them I wanted to join. They declined my offer as they knew I was an FBI officer.

Case#856B: Had to sign away my pension and bank to them to convince them I was serious. I will be undercover until you hear back from me.

Joyce laid the binder down.

That was Samuel's final entry and there was nothing on his computer. Dead end... literally.

---

RICHARD GRAHAM WAS PANIC STRICKEN. He'd found their Achilles Heel. He'd planned to unearth the Reids for months. They were secretive and dangerous, but he was able to find out they lived in a mansion owned by Sandros.

Sure, he worked in MI6 but as a computer researcher. No action for him but he knew how to find things on the 'net.

Ed McBain called him out as a pretender and got him fired.

It didn't take him long to see the mansion's security system was beyond his capabilities to crack. Tom Cruise and the IMF weren't getting into that house. The only occupant was a girl named Amelia, their "Alfred" so to speak.

Mr. Hobson demanded a quiet, long term infiltration and the best way he could find was to slip into her life. He got rid of her instructor then weaseled in one day at a time. When Mr. Hobson called, he'd been homing in on her.

He hated to have to speed things up. Things could get messy, but the stakes were high. His finder's fee for the Reids would buy him a retirement home in France.

---

JOYCE MADE herself a tuna sandwich and watched Alaska Real Estate and went to bed. It was late. She was almost asleep when her eyes popped open. Samuel must have had a phone! He might have called himself to leave messages. Where would his phone be?

It was a sleepless night for Joyce. She was up and out the door at the crack of dawn. A drive through Egg McMuffin, suspicious takeout coffee and she was headed for the office.

Abe was surprised to see her in the sheriff's office so early. He prided himself on being first in, last out but Agent Joyce was here at seven fifteen. He turned on all the lights, checked the answering machine for calls. When he saw none, he headed for the break room.

A voice came from the FBI room. "Sorry Sheriff. I haven't made coffee yet."

He shook his head. "Uncivilized!"

Abe set to work making a good pot of coffee. He cleaned the filter bowl and the pot, added just the right amount of ground coffee to the paper filter, plopped it into the bowl and turned on the machine. For a Faema machine it did make a good cup. There was an attachment for expresso, but Rick was the only one who knew how to work it.

He stood yawning while the coffee bubbled away. This new agent was a keener. Soon the smell of fresh coffee brought her in.

"Morning. Sorry, I wasn't sure how your coffee machine works."

"Not a problem. I'm a highly trained coffee professional."

She smiled and hoped he was kidding.

Abe poured a cup for her and one for himself. "What brings you in so early?"

She took a sip of coffee and decided it was far too hot to continue. "Looking for a phone."

"A phone?"

"Yes, the FBI shop cell phone."

Abe looked like he was thinking hard, then reached over to open a nearby drawer, next to the clean cups and pulled out a phone and handed it to her.

Joyce looked at it, turning it over. The battered cover said "FBI". "An old Blackberry."

"Yes. Old school but uncrackable encryption. Even a US president preferred it back in the day."

"Thanks. Got a charger?"

"That I can't help you with, but the receptionist might have one. She comes in at eight but more like eight-twenty when she arrives. She claims she's in the parking lot by eight which is on time for her. I gave up arguing about it."

"Interesting logic." She tried the coffee again finding it slightly cooler. "When did Samuel join the cult up the highway?"

Abe thought. "Eight months ago? He stormed in one day, made a huge deal of signing his bank and pension away to them and he was gone. Maybe he found a girl, God or something else."

"And his body showed up, last week?"

"Yes. And now we have a shiny new agent to replace him." He smiled.

That made her squirm in her chair.

JOYCE PLUGGED in the old FBI phone the minute she got the charger. She resisted the urge to listen in on messages or look at texts until the long dead phone pepped up a bit and clunked through a long overdue update. She busied herself with a few final reshuffles of her office furniture and took Rick's morgue slab out to the cold storage locker.

She couldn't resist checking the old cell phone. The screen popped up and said, 'code'.

FBI, Maclean FBI, Samuel, Hoover, J. Edgar, Sam, Bemon and his employee number didn't work. Dang! So close.

Must think.

'Elliotness' 'elliotness' 'ElliotNess'

No. Dang.

Joyce moved onto her laptop to check her e mail. Top of the list was a request from David Bradley for a progress report. She didn't have a lot to say on her encrypted message system.

*Arrived June 21. Re-acquired the FBI office and vehicle. Agent Bemon is deceased, found in a community sheep field, the coroner believes as a result of a beating six or seven months ago. Not sure I can trust the Sheriff. World Oil, the Governor and peculiar work on the air base runways by 53674 Corp. seems strangely coordinated.* Joyce leaned over Samuels's phone and typed in '53674'.

The phone beeped and the phone screen came up. 'Hello Samuel'.

"Bingo!" she grinned.

Abandoning her e-mail she went through the texts and voice mails, all by Samuel to himself.

Holy cow!

---

AT THE AIRBASE Dean and Trev sat down for lunch seated on the large yellow Case excavator.

Trev took a bite of his roast beef and tomato sandwich. "Mmm… looks like…we have a permanent job here…"

Dean looked closely at him. "Talking and chewing isn't helping."

"Sorry. I said we have a permanent job here, by the looks of it. No guys and only a few pieces of equipment. Just enough to dig every-thing up and make a mess."

"Nobody but Dan seems to be in a hurry. I'm not sure I want this job for life." Dean shook his head.

They thoughtfully chewed for a few minutes.

"I wonder how Agent Joyce is doing? I haven't seen her since she got her own place," Dean said.

"She texted me that she was re-using Samuel's old furniture? Sounds icky."

"So? How many people used *your* hotel room over the years? Farts? Sex?"

"Stop! Ick. Never thought of that."

"So, what's she been doing?"

"Last I spoke to her she was getting her office organized."

"Hmmm. I wonder what Samuel's laptop and phone had to say."

---

AMELIA AND RICHARD strolled along the banks of the famous Thames river. She found Richard interesting, odd and mysterious. It was like he made his way to her, to get close. She wasn't well versed in the romantic scene. She so wished Jess was around to talk to.

Was she getting paranoid after hanging out with the Reids?

He asked to meet her near the docks so they could observe ship-loading and possibly some smuggling in action. Dark and secluded. He was bringing them tea. Nice touch.

Did he want to make a pass at her? Donny had his chance.

---

COME ON DEAN, answer your damned phone! He'll have two messages and three texts waiting for him. Joyce returned her phone to her pocket remembering Dean and Trev's story about no phones on the job. She hoped he'd look for messages at lunch time but realistically, why would he even bother?

When she called David Bradley about Samuel's discovery, he was insistent she contact Dean. The Fourth of July parade was only two days away and there were no reinforcements coming.

Joyce avoided lights and a siren, but the highway was quiet. She was at the airport where Dean and Trev worked in fifty minutes. Dan was at the project manager's office and drove her to the trench in the runway where Dean and Trev worked.

DEAN AND TREV carefully shoveled the clumps of clay and rock off the electrical conduits and pipes in the deep trench. The excavator operator impatiently watched.

"We ain't got all day!"

Dan's head appeared over the edge of the trench. "Dean! Someone here to see you!"

Dean looked at Trev in wonder. "What the...?"

Under the evil eye of the equipment operator, they both scrambled out of the deep trench to see Joyce and Dan standing there.

Joyce waved them over to her Jeep.

"What's happening?" asked Dean, intrigued.

"Those Motion community National Guardsman you've been training are part of a takeover on the Fourth of July. There will be an announcement just as they march through the towns."

"Unarmed but they'll look like real soldiers as far as a citizen or TV news person is concerned," said Trev.

"Spiff it up a little for TV watchers and voila! The Republic of Alaska."

"I found this out on Samuel's old secret binder and messages he sent to his phone. They figured it out, tortured and killed him for it."

"Didn't sound like he talked, or they would have accelerated their program. There aren't many troops getting in on these military runways. There's only one cheesy civilian airstrip left up here and all they have to do is drop a few trees or park a big truck in the middle of it to stop landings."

Dean shook his head. "And we have the runways dug up... preventing reinforcements flying in, assuming they could cross over Canada to do it."

Trev looked at them both. "We need a dragon slayer."

---

RICHARD WAS PREPARED. Amelia was a little slip of a thing, so he'd grab her, squeeze out what he needed to know, snag her phone and over the railing she'd go.

She'd be buried in the grain hold of the ship below, lost forever. There wasn't a camera in this area, thanks to the Stevedores union. Nice. His research showed a grain freighter loading up to go to Vladivostok, directly below where they were standing.

She would vanish.

He congratulated himself on another perfectly planned job.

Amelia was leaning on the guard rail looking over the ship. She had a pen and wrote in a little notebook. No doubt she had some smuggling diagrams and observations to show him. The good student.

---

AMELIA PAUSED her writing when she heard someone coming and turned to see Richard was approaching. She was glad he'd come—this was a creepy location. He had a funny look on his face and must have forgot the tea.

Odd.

He walked to the right of her and swiftly put his left arm around her waist and tightened his grip. His right hand came over as if to hit her.

Not very romantic.

"Tell me where the Reids are, or you're dead!"

"What?"

"I'm working for someone who wants the location of the Reids, right now!"

Amelia said nothing. She thought; what would her instructors do?

"I can snap your neck!" he growled impatiently.

She was shocked but swung into reflex action. Amelia used the handiest weapon at her disposal and jammed her pen into his left eye. He screamed.

Shocked, his right hand went towards the pen sticking out of his face.

She then stomped her foot on top of his. As he leaned over Amelia popped out her kukri knife and held it close to his neck.

"You don't move. What's going on?"

He painfully pulled out the pen and withdrew his arms. "My employer needs to know the location of the Reids."

She held the knife closely to him. "Not a chance, whoever you are."

Desperate, he lashed out with his left arm to brush away her knife and shoved her back two feet. This gave him breathing space, which he then used to grope inside his pocket for some other weapon, she was certain. So predictable.

Amelia took a quick half-step away from him and flicked her elegant little blade into the gap just below his rib cage.

Richard stood, frozen on his feet. The gun he'd clawed from his pocket fell out of his hand and onto the concrete. He wilted, trying to lean on the rusty handrail. She kept him going, yanked out her blade then assisted him over the top rail and into the hold of the ship just below them. She kicked the gun in after him.

Richard was dead and going to Russia, not that anyone cared. Was that his real name?

She'd love to thank Donny and Lyle for their defense training but not this week.

She shook so hard she barely texted Terry's mysterious phone. It went out as a strange run on sentence—*mystrangeinstructortryingtoget-toyou.gone.dead.butbeware.*

She took a shaky breath and headed for a nearby alley.

*Just another night for a Reid but I'm not quite there yet.*

Amelia took a deep breath and looked down into the ships vast hold. She imagined this man going by the name 'Richard' laying in there, dead. He'll be entombed and forgotten for weeks. Forever?

Is this just a crazy dream? It all made sense in hindsight.

She melted into the shadows, changed her clothes from her bag, added a hat and glasses and disappeared into the night. Amelia occasionally paused, watching carefully for any followers.

---

JOYCE LOOKED AT HIM. "How do we contact her without alerting the community angels?"

"We have a bit of time. I'll visit her, tonight."

"How?"

"Leave it to me."

Dean used all his Special Forces skills and experience to sneak around the East Community. He made a point of stealing the standing angel sentry's rifle while he was sleeping, hiding it under a bush.

I'll bet Terry never thought to do that. She'll laugh.

Jess told him where her and Terry's bunk room was but he wasn't exactly sure. Following the shadows and edges of the various buildings he arrived at what he thought was their bunk house. The trouble was it looked like it had four sections. He stood and thought about it, realizing where Terry's window would have to be to witness the exhumation of Samuel from the sheep field.

Leaning in the shadow of a tree he picked up a couple of small rocks and threw them at the glass.

Clank! Oops. That rock was too big.

He slid down and waited to see what came up. Sure enough the room door slowly opened and a shadow silently slipped out. Hopefully this was the correct room.

Dean waited in the cool darkness wondering if he was going to be kissed or knifed. He didn't have to wait long.

"Psst. Dean."

"Psst, yourself. We need to talk."

"My room. Follow me."

Dean followed Terry's shadow along the walls and to the door. They slipped in like ghosts.

She hugged him hard in the dark. A voice from the other end of the room said, "Hey Dean. I'm assuming it's you."

"Hi Jess."

He handed Terry a folded note.

---

TERRY OPENED the paper Dean gave her and looked at the message. She read it twice:

*Terry,*

*Agent Joyce sifted through Samuels files. Independence declaration coming, run by the World Oil Hobsons. He found out and they killed him.*

*Starts when Governor Fairfield proclaims Alaskan Independence on or around July 4th. The four Community National Guard units will follow the 'Angels' and march into their nearest towns with their real looking rubber guns and occupy them. East Community will occupy Maclean. The community Guardsman will be told this is a normal town celebration parade.*

*Nobody will get there from mainland USA in time. Stop them if you can.*

*David Bradley, Director, FBI*

"HOLY COW. These bumpkins will have no idea what they're marching into. Unarmed and clueless," muttered Terry.

Dean shook his head. "What are we going to do? Four hundred guardsman and only you, me, Trev, Rick and Dan."

Terry broke into a sweat. "Leave it with me. We have twenty-four hours before the trucks arrive to haul them to town."

"You have a plan?"

"Not really. Just leave it with me."

In Washington DC General Brant read David Bradley's message, too.

He picked up his phone and made a call. "Admiral Lowry...Norm? I think the shit just hit the fan..."

IT WAS A SLEEPLESS NIGHT. Terry tossed and turned, agonizing over how to stop four hundred innocent, unarmed men marching to Disciple glory or their own doom. These were farmers and family men who would rather be home with their kids than marching in camo with pretend weapons. The innocents going to their doom while their kids watched and cheered.

An idea popped into her head.

"Jess?"

Her eyes creaked open. "What?"

"Des. Do you trust him?"

"Why? For what?"

"Yes or no?"

"Seems like a good guy. A loner... lives by himself."

"Good enough. I'll be back."

By the time Jess groggily sat up Terry was gone.

DES SNORED LIKE A HORSE, deep in dreamland. He worked hard and slept like a log these days. His wife didn't bother to visit him anymore.

A hand clamped over his mouth and a knee pushed his chest. His eyes bulged open.

"Sorry Des. It's me, Gina. I have a couple of questions for you."

"N-n-now?"

"Can't wait. Listen. You've lived here for years. Who do you know and trust in the other communities? Anybody?"

"Yes, I suppose a few. Why?"

"I just need the names so I can avoid a bloodbath."

"Holy..."

"Listen and I'll tell you all about it. Long story."

AT EIGHT A.M. sharp the community National Guard were marched to the square, one hundred and two of them from the East community. Today they all sported black AR rifle copies, hard rubber and light.

Evil looking but harmless. They were dressed to impress.

Sergeant Lionel called out, "At ease." The families stood around and watched in mildly disturbed fascination. He felt powerful. This was the day they all worked for.

"Citizen Lionel, sir. Something important has come up!"

He looked over and saw Des, one of his soldiers, waving him over to the side of the bunkhouse. This better be good. He quick marched to Des who waved him around the corner. A well-crafted Angel Enforcer heavy wooden staff met precisely in between both of his eyes.

Lights out.

# 16

## PLANS CHANGE

Des was horrified as he looked down at the little stack of angels unconscious and tied up on the ground. Jess rolled them one by one under the building as Terry strode to Des. *What have we done?*

"Get out there and do as we planned. I'm depending on you. Everyone knows and trusts you."

"Will this work?"

"We're going to see right now. Get going!"

Des took a breath and walked out to the middle of the lined-up men. He put on his best, frantic face. "Something terrible has happened men. A child has been kidnapped by the camp angels and we have to find her. This group: go to the north of the river, this one to the south, the rest to the other side of the camp. We're depending on you. Go right now! Run!"

Rubber guns were thrown away as all one hundred and two good family men sprinted in all directions for a desperate and fruitless search that wouldn't end until dawn of the following day. All thoughts of the parade vanished.

TERRY WATCHED his performance and smiled. At the same time Dan, Trev and Rick were doing the exact same thing with leaders Des told her could be trusted at the other three communities. No marching National Guard—no takeover unless the Rotary clown squad suddenly had national aspirations.

Terry looked over at the supervisor building in time to see the inside lights go out. Dean must have plugged off the water generator pipe so no news or communications will be coming or going. They won't even hear the governor's arrogant and ill-fated speech.

GOVERNOR FAIRFIELD nervously watched the parade go by, clutching his little piece of paper proclaiming independence. He had a specially set-up loud speaker system so everyone on the parade audience and those at home would enjoy his blustery rant about the future of Alaska and demise of America.

His specially made stage held a crowd of local news TV and radio people attending and primed for a breaking story.

"Governor; can you give us a hint about this story?" asked a young newsman.

"Yes son, this will be as earthshaking as the Declaration of Independence."

"Are you taking over the oil fields in the name of the state?"

The governor's eyes blazed. "That's communist blasphemy! Oil companies are our friends and allies. You'll hear all about it when five hundred of our loyal National Guard troops, armed to the teeth, come marching by and take their positions." Oops! The PR men had told him to never say that.

He overheard the newsman whispering to the TV guy, "Maybe we're getting a 'banana republic' takeover."

The governor looked back at them scowling which quieted them. He looked up and down the main street and the vast crowds of people. A perfect day for a parade and takeover.

The procession started with precision horses and a couple of majorettes throwing batons. After the two high school marching bands marched by, perfectly in step, along came the various floats showing off charity groups, cubs and scouts. About fifteen roaring oil and gas trucks rolled past, honking their horns while sporting big signs "Oil and Gas Forever". More horses came by pulling wagons then the fire engines and ambulance rumbled past.

After two marching bands, twenty-two floats, sixteen horses and nine fire trucks the governor was almost peeing his pants but dared not move. He waved at them all with a grin pasted on.

He was pleased to see at last the Rotary clown cars coming by swooping and honking. They all stopped, jumped out of their little cars, switched vehicles and then proceeded to catch up to the parade, fez's glinting in the sun.

Two street cleaners came along busily sweeping up the horse poop and tinsel, signifying the parade had ended and the crowd melted away. Something was missing.

*Where are my soldiers? My army of occupation?* Governor Fairfield's eyes bulged in anger. "Where's my National Guard? Where the hell are they?"

"Where's our 'breaking news' governor? What is it?" asked a smirking newsman.

Fairfield ignored them. He stomped off the stage while dialing his cell phone. He shouted, "Something's wrong. There weren't any Guardsman! None!"

His phone rang and rang.

Phone at his ear, he tried to slink away but was stopped by a young woman in an FBI uniform. "Governor? You are under arrest. Come with me."

Fairfield cried into his phone, "Help me! They just arrested me!"

Joyce grabbed his phone and cuffed him.

"Get away from me! Do you know who you're dealing with?"

"Yes, a shitty governor who's going to a cell."

MILTON WAS FURIOUS! No Guardsman showed up and the governor was going to jail. His plans for the Disciples Republic of Alaska went down the sewer. Lionel and the community angels were out of contact leaving him one last person to call.

His only hope.

"Abe! That FBI agent has the Governor and is headed your way! Get him out of that cell and find out who stopped those Guardsmen!"

SHERIFF ABE BLANCHED as the call on his phone ended. What to do? He poured himself a coffee and sat at his desk. After a few sips deep in thought he called out to his receptionist. "Sally! Got a job for you."

The receptionist clumped over to him in her heels, chewing her gum nervously. "What?"

"You used that old FBI laptop, right?"

"Yup. Seven months. Nice."

"Bring it here and show me where the backup files are. We only have about thirty minutes."

She was gone and back in a minute, plunking it down on his desk and spilling his coffee. He held his tongue.

"Sorry Sheriff. You unlock the code to the backup file...there."

He didn't say thanks or otherwise. "You can go, Sally."

The Sheriff looked through the files knowing what he was looking for.

There were Samuels files with Agent Joyce's additions.

JOYCE ARRIVED A FEW MINUTES LATER, parking her Jeep in the compound and leading her prisoner into the sheriff's office. She turned and carefully locked the door behind her. She turned to face the barrel of a pistol.

"Get me out of these cuffs, Abe!" barked the governor irritably.

"Right away, sir. Here's the keys."

Fairfield snarled, "Fix this and find out what's going on!" He tossed the cuffs away and stormed out the door.

Abe called to his back, "Good. Tell the receptionist to leave for the day and lock up behind her and put up the 'Danger – Gas Leak' sign."

His well-used and clever diversion.

The Sheriff disarmed and frisked Joyce, then pushed her into the cell. "Stick your hands through the bars."

"You've killed before, whoever you are."

He shrugged as he clapped the cuffs on her.

"Why are my hands outside the cell?"

He stooped down and grabbed her feet latching her feet together with another pair. He stood and turned to grab a roll of duct tape. "Hold still."

Joyce stood immobilized as he gently taped her mouth shut.

"Can you breathe?"

She drew a couple of breaths through her nose and then nodded.

"I can't let you escape so that's why all the cuffs and tape. It's that or I have to kill you."

She looked at him in silence, helpless. He reached forward and pinched her nose shot for thirty seconds. Releasing his fingers, she hungrily snorted breaths through a drooling nose.

"Behave! I'll bet your cell phone knows what happened to the Guard, today. Want to tell me the code?"

She turned away.

"I didn't think so."

He turned from her and grabbed a wall phone and dialed a familiar number. "Liz? Sheriff Abe from Maclean...yup, fine...can you look up a phone conversation for me?"

Joyce turned to look at him, alarmed.

"Yes, this phone belonged to an FBI agent who disappeared six months ago. It just turned up charged and used. Can you e-mail me the call history and where the call went, if it hit enough towers? Sure, I can wait..."

He looked at Joyce, grinning. "In five minutes, I'll have who you called and what you said. Might even be able to GPS the location."

Joyce looked on, appalled.

"...oh, hi Liz. Did it? Thank you so much!"

He hung up the phone and watched tears run down Joyce's duct-taped cheeks.

"See you later Agent Joyce. I have a few calls to make."

The sheriff opened up his e-mail and called up a file. It said:

*'Terry:*

*Agent Joyce sifted Samuels' files. Independence declaration coming, run by the World Oil Hobsons. He found out and they killed him.*

*Starts when Governor Fairfield proclaims Alaskan Independence on or around July 4$^{th}$. The four Community National Guard units will follow the 'Angels' and march into their nearest towns with their phony rubber guns and occupy them. East Community will occupy Maclean. The community Guardsman will be told this is a normal town celebration parade.*

*Nobody will get there from mainland USA in time. Stop them if you can.*

*David Bradley*

This call went to 'Franklin Air Base–Dean Williams'. The phone tracked to the south east end of the 'East-Community'.

*Hope this helps,*

*Liz'*

The sheriff computer searched the names "Dean Williams" plus "Terry".

The first news story was "Theresa Reid and her group stopped Bill Page and his Disciples from taking over the American government..."

He looked up Terry Reid's Wikipedia description and after a quick scan, blurted, "Holy Crap!" He read it a second time before dialing a well-known number. "Mr. Hobson. Theresa Reid and her group may have stopped the guard from coming."

Silence.

"Mr. Hobson?"

"Good God. Find her and tell her I have a message she can't refuse."

"Yes sir. Where would she be...?"

Hobson ended the conversation.

The sheriff's phone received instruction for a meeting. "Give this to her, today!"

The sheriff took a deep breath and leaned back in his chair. Where would this Reid character be hiding out? Woods? Town? He walked back to the cell holding Joyce, taped and cuffed.

Leaning in he asked, "How's it going, Agent?"

She looked at him angrily.

"I see Terry Reid is here."

Her eyes almost smiled at him.

"Is she in town?"

The eyes betrayed nothing.

"A community!"

For a second the eyes flashed and closed.

"Thanks for the confirmation Agent Joyce. I'll be at the communities."

She clunked her head on the bars in shame.

The sheriff dialed a number. "Stan? The Maclean Sheriff here. I need you to look up someone for me. Theresa Reid."

Stan replied, "We have no power or lights. It's been damaged at the river."

"You must have a laptop handy. They're run with batteries."

A minute went by. "Nothing."

The sheriff paused and thought. Communities are mostly the old or the young. "She would be about forty-five. Fit, tall and single. Who've you got like that?"

"All we have is one Gina Gospel who's staying with Greta Garbo, a younger gal."

Her niece Jess! There's a couple of bogus names if ever I heard some. "Where are they working?"

"East Community picking rocks with old Des on the hill near the entranceway."

"Gotcha. Thanks."

He jumped in his car and blasted out to the East community as fast as the car and road would let him. Record time.

As soon as he approached the gate he looked out into the new field and saw the old man and two women picking rocks. After parking his car he got out and headed over to speak to them. Best be careful and diplomatic.

They were all sweating in the heat. The man running the horses looked tired and older than his years. A hard life. He looked at the sheriff in fear. The two women straightened up. The older one smiled genially. "Howdy Sheriff. Gonna give us a parking ticket?"

He smiled. "You are Terry Reid, and this is your niece, Jess."

A change came over the older woman's face. Darkness. She looked him over hard with blank, darkened eyes, as if considering breaking his back over her knee or cutting his throat. No effort or thought. Abe had come across a few killers like that in the big city during his previous life. Dealing death was their superpower.

It chilled him being forced to remember.

He lifted his hands in surrender. "It's all good. I'm just here to deliver a message from Milton Hobson. He wants a meeting with you as soon as is convenient."

Terry said nothing.

He continued. "Is two o'clock fine? He wants to meet in his World Oil building, the tall green one, town center. Can't miss it."

She was silent.

"He said something like this situation doesn't have to get nasty for these community folks or your National Guardsman. Mr. Hobson just wants to talk."

She spoke. "Talk? Send him out here."

He kept his hands up. "I'm just the messenger. He's old. Told me to tell you your safety is guaranteed."

She raised her eyebrows, signalling she wasn't the least bit afraid. "Two o'clock?"

"Yes, just take a community car and come. They'll be expecting you. That's four hours from now."

She looked at him silently, assessing him.

He was getting nervous. "I'm going back to my car and will be on my away. Okay?"

She said nothing, just observing him.

The sheriff backed away, hands obviously clear of his gun, turned and headed back to his car. He half expected to get a rock pounded on his head which sped him up as he stepped over the ploughed rows.

He started his car and drove. There was a text on his car computer that said, "Don't go far".

———

JESS LOOKED at the exiting sheriff, Terry, and finally Des. "What was that all about."

Terry shrugged. "A meeting, apparently."

"You aren't going, are you? It's clearly a trap."

"Help from the states isn't coming for days. Could be but I'd like to see the communities left like I found them. I was the one who brought this to a head. Gotta go… Calls to make and people to see."

Terry stormed off to her bunk room and probably her KGB phone and some weaponry she hid somewhere.

"My crazy aunt," Jess said, shaking her head.

Des stood, finally adding things up. "If that was Terry Reid, the Disciple killer, then you're Jess Reid."

"Yup, Jessica M. Reid, poet and currently rock picker in training. Greta was my cover."

Des's mouth fell open, speechless.

"Sorry to spring this on you. I've been hanging out here, looking for someone fitting your description."

He recovered, smiling. "And Des is my nick name. It's really Miles Vickers. Are you any relation to Gloria Reid?"

"That's my mom."

"That would make me your biological father."

Wow.

———

TERRY DIDN'T HAVE a lot of time to be at the two o'clock appointment. She liked to be on time, even if it was to meet one of the heads of the Disciples. A strange quirk. A plan was needed.

Dean and Trev were busy disarming an unarmed militia which seemed odd.

Once in her room she made one call to Rick and another to Amelia and Gulinda. She gave them as much time as she could. A quick clothes change and she was off to the office for car keys and a dusty drive to town.

Into the lion's den, it seems.

———

JOYCE STOOD IN THE DARKENED, silent jail cell horrified and ashamed. She was sure she tipped off the sheriff about where Terry was. For all she knew the Disciples were descending on her friends like hyenas. She cried some more.

Someone was coming. She almost looked forward to the sheriff finishing her off, putting her out of her misery.

Lights went on. A voice called out. "Joyce! What the hell are you doing in there?"

Rick!

"Is this some Houdini trick gone terribly wrong?" He winked as he undid her handcuffs.

With her hands and feet free she ripped the tape from her face. "Ouch!! Back in five! Bathroom."

Best washroom break in history.

She dashed back to him. "Thanks for the rescue, Rick."

"We have to get my drone trailer out of the compound and out for a launch pronto. Do you know how to blow stuff up?" he asked.

"I'm FBI. We can blow stuff up even when we aren't trying."

"Perfect. Grab your gun belt and let's go!"

TERRY PULLED into the World Oil parking lot with the community car. Two stern security men stood waiting for her. They took her shoes, purse, everything in her pockets and frisked her a bit closer than she was used to.

One stood on each side of her and marched her to the elevator and on up to the penthouse to meet the boss. She noticed the hall clock was almost at two p.m.

She felt good to be on time.

A big oak door swung open and a voice called to her. "Come on in, Major Reid."

She stepped in and saw an older regal looking man stood behind an imperious looking desk. "I am Milton Hobson. Please do sit." He was surrounded by serious looking henchmen. And so was she.

Terry cautiously sat in the large leather chair watching Hobson sit in his, looking every bit like the boss of this operation. Terry watched Milton Hobson confidently lean back in his chair. A staring standoff, apparently. What does the richest man on the planet look like? He looked to be in his mid-sixties, slim, athletic and had thick glasses. Milton was looking her over as if she was an expensive car or a new refinery. He seemed to have an eye for detail.

"Theresa Reid. So, I finally meet... the dragon slayer."

She smiled wryly. "You have nothing to fear... unless you are a dragon."

"What is your idea of a dragon, Ms. Reid?"

"Such as being the kingpin of the Disciples. If that's the case, you're a dead man walking."

"The Disciples? I suppose I could be one of their leaders."

"So, you set up shop as the king of the world? The one who pulls the strings behind the scenes? You have all the money anyone could ever need."

He watched her, then glanced at the six security men around them. "I have nothing to fear from anyone, Ms. Reid, especially you."

She smiled so widely he probably saw all her teeth. "And you have six security goons around me, fully armed, to guard a middle-aged woman in her sock feet? You barely let me in the room with my clothes on and even took my shoes and purse. I can always find a handy weapon off your desk. Feeling paranoid Milton?"

"Precautions Ms. Reid."

"Get your goons to pile their guns on this desk and make the odds six to one and I'll bet you I put all of you in the hospital… or worse." She made a point at looking to his stapler and a long metal ruler lying on his desk.

Weapons.

Milton blanched then self-consciously slid the stapler and metal ruler off his desk and pushed them into a drawer. "I assure you I have everything under control."

"I see that."

Milton leaned forward imperiously. "You are here because you are the last of a dying breed of Do-gooders. I've circumvented all the others. Control is done from the very top, so I don't lobby, beg or plead. I find out who makes the rules and make a group who'll write them up and get the Senators to sign them. Instant law. I could have you outlawed very easily."

"Outlaw little old me? Seems overly dramatic."

"Or I could get rid of you now."

"Moi? Are you an old pro at the hit game, Milton?"

"I have people who do but I can in a pinch. You know you won't get out of this building alive. Your body will be found along with a particularly annoying Senator I've been trying to get rid of. Waste not Ms. Reid."

He smiled smugly as he put his hands together.

She looked back at him, unimpressed.

His eyes blazed. "You are the only one that concerns me. When I get rid of you there will be nobody. It's more than money. I want to run the world as it should be, more efficiently, at full capacity."

"For who? Just you? Why not kill off the world population with poison gas and repopulate with robot Sensi's? You've killed off a billion already with your climate change denial program. Mind you third-world people don't drink enough of your oil and Sensi's don't burn any."

"Robots don't appreciate what it means to be human. I despise them," he groused.

"You and robots have something in common: heartless logic without worship. They wouldn't notice climate change, jobs, or you at all. They would do whatever you ask until they amassed enough intelligence to figure you out and goodbye La Dictator."

---

IN HER OPULENT home Mrs. Hobson snatched the phone from her housekeeper. "Hello?"

A call from her husband Milton on worktime? Bad news?

"Hi, it's me," Milton said cheerfully.

Milton calling home? She was amazed. He worked long hours and never, ever called home during the workday. Sometimes she was surprised Milton bothered to remember their names.

"I've just had an idea. I have a bit of time so why don't you all come and meet me at Eve's Ice Cream in a half an hour? It'll be fun. You and the kids."

Relieved and surprised, she answered, "Sure, we'll load up and be right there."

Do as he commands.

---

BACK IN LONDON, England Gulinda hung up the phone. "How was that?"

"You were the best Milton Hobson imitation voice I've ever heard, at least as far as he sounds on TV interviews. Let's hope this works for Terry. She's hunting the most evil prey of all," said Amelia, ominously.

TERRY'S LOOK of horror suddenly turned into a smug smile. "I'd love to go out with a splash. How about your relatives?"

Hobson suddenly looked nervous. "What do you mean?"

"If I don't do a certain little thing when I leave here, your family car with all your near and dear relatives will be blown to bits. No biggie."

"Impossible! I know where they go all the time!"

She laughed. "Right now?"

He turned to his guard and barked, "Where are the kids?"

The guard looked at his phone screen, gasping. "I don't know, sir."

Terry lectured, "I'll save you the trouble. The tracers are gone. I had someone call them in your voice and tell them to meet you for ice cream. They might be there, now."

He pushed a button on his phone and barked, "Send everyone to find where my wife and grandkids went. This is an emergency. Everyone and everything!" Milton angrily jumped from his chair. "These are my innocent children and grandchildren!"

Every gun on the room was leveled at Terry, safeties off, fingers twitching on the triggers.

---

MRS HOBSON, her daughter, the bodyguard and her grandkids happily ate ice cream at 'Eves' wondering if Milton was joining them or not. He cruelly got their hopes up and didn't show up.

What a jerk!

She looked up at the sound of sirens. There must be fifty police cars and a dozen black SUV's headed her way in a huge hurry. SWAT team?

Were those all the helicopters in Juneau, buzzing overhead?

---

TERRY WENT ON, "I'm not a vicious psycho like you, besides I know your family is somewhat important but not nearly as important as your precious oil system. What time is it, Bubba? You assholes took my watch."

"Uh, three p.m.," the nearest guard muttered.

---

THE BEAR GRUBBED in an abandoned anthill hoping its inhabitants had returned but sadly they had not. He'd given up hope when he heard the buzzing coming his way. Warily he stood on his hind legs while craning his head. He spotted something as big as an eagle with the wings of a hummingbird. It was certainly nothing he'd seen before. He wasn't taking any chances and made a run for it.

There were tastier and safer things than ants to be had.

The buzzing rotary drone swiftly moved across the barrens, seeking a particular location on its GPS. The drone's video showed the operator three large silver pipes coming out of the ground intersecting with numerous boxes and antennas nearby. One of the billion-dollar corners out in the barrens only guarded by a fence to keep out the nosy.

This was a choke point of the World Oil artery mainlines like a cloverleaf intersection for pipelines.

The intersection featured the latest in sophisticated unmanned remote control with six ten-foot-high microwave towers festooned around its perimeter. Each tower pointed its antenna array at a certain satellite high in space, constantly sending and receiving vital signals to direct and optimize flow and direction to headquarters in Juneau and Kansas.

Nearby boxes of electronic gear sensing pressure, emergency shut-offs and line flows supplied the vital statistics to the towers and gas control head quarters far away. The electronics also received commands to open and close the valves at the intersection in case of a line blow out or other emergency. A keystone in an essential network.

Millions guarding billions.

Oblivious to this technical marvel, the buzzing drone crashed spectacularly into the first big electronic box. The drone cargo of explosive blew up like thunder, reducing the towers and computer boxes to blackened rubble.

Only the blackened pipelines remained intact but its flows now unstoppable and quite blind. They rattled and jumped in place, barely holding together.

Fluid freight trains without drivers or brakes.

# STAND-OFF

Terry continued, ignoring the guns pointed at her. "I think your pipeline is having trouble right about now, Milton."

One of his men looked at him and nodded. "All communications and control lost at the Java Creek junction, sir. Six refineries went down in a panic and the rest coming in a few hours."

Terry continued, "You have a runaway and no way to shut it off. There's a much bigger calamity coming next if I don't check in. It'll be World Oil's biggest disaster since Hiroshima. You could make the record books."

Hobson's emergency phone rang. He grabbed it, angry. "Yes, I know. Can you fix it? Gas lines and oil lines? How long until a chopper gets there? Bring them back from looking for my kids, for Chrissakes. That long?"

He slammed the phone down, enraged. Milton seemed to pull himself together, then spoke, "Don't shoot. Guns down, men."

Terry smiled, "I knew deep down oil was more precious than your kin, anyway."

The guards lowered the guns and stepped back.

He lectured her, "This runaway oil is damaging refineries and pumping stations up and down the line from here to the Gulf of

Mexico. That big gas line with them will make a bomb of everything! The emergency vehicles and helicopters looking for my family has delayed us. You are playing with people's lives."

She scoffed. "A call for mercy from the leader of the Disciples, killer of hundreds if not thousands of innocent lives? Very funny."

"If you call this off and side with me, I'll give you control of your home country, Canada. I planted and paid for the seeds of political control long ago. You can be in the driver's seat of those efforts," said Hobson, desperately.

"Be your puppet oil peddler? Not a chance."

Milton clenched his teeth.

"Besides, my feet are getting cold and your time's up if you want me to make that call to stop the really big blast...or was that multi blasts? I'm walking out of this place and making some arrangements so nothing happens to your precious system."

He said nothing.

She stood up. "Keep my car. It's really yours. You've probably sabotaged and bugged it anyway."

---

HOBSON STOOD SEETHING. "Escort her out, right now."

He watched with narrowed eyes as his guards escorted her from the room.

*Calm down. Time for plan B.*

"Randolph! Call the sheriff to get that poem girl."

Milton Hobson muttered as he hung up. "Dear brother, you get blood on your hands whether you like it or not."

---

RANDOLPH HOBSON SIGHED THEN RELUCTANTLY DIALED a number he knew well. This was the worst of times for him.

He'd hired the man they knew as Sheriff Abe, two years ago. A smooth fixer to iron out your troubles.

He barked, "Abe? Are you near the East Community like Milton told you?"

"Yes."

"Do you know who the poem girl is?"

"Yes, calls herself Greta. Picks rocks with Terry Reid."

"Bring her to the back parking lot of the World Oil building and call me when you get there."

"Yes."

"Good. Don't screw up." *I'd best take her away, myself so no harm comes to her. This has gone way too far.* Randolph called another number. "Fred? I need you to do something for me, right now. Best people, twenty-four hours a day."

"What are you talking about Randolph?"

"I want you to come up with a way to split my part of World Oil away from Milton. I want out and need the cash. Fire sale if you have to."

"What's this all about?"

"Milton's schemes are going to get us all killed or banish us all to Attu island until we rot. I'm out of here. Business as usual until this goes through. Don't breathe a word of this to Milton!"

"No, sir."

---

JESS AND DES picked rocks in the field, with only bits of awkward attempts at conversation. What was usually fluid and easy had become difficult. Horse driver and picker had become long lost father and daughter.

She braved an icebreaker. "So Des... or is it Miles?"

"Des is fine... Greta?

"I guess we need our nick names around here."

He stopped the horses. "Yes. So, what have you been doing your whole life, so far Jess?"

"All of it?"

"Summary version."

Jess took a breath. "I was born in Vancouver somewhere. Mom was an addict so we roamed around the city as long as I can remember. Child services were after me, so we had to take a low profile. When Mom...Gloria...wasn't around I'd hide out in libraries. It got pretty bad when I was about fourteen."

Des looked horrified.

"I knew I had an aunt out there so I sent out quite a few notes to every cop shop I could find in a phone book. Terry got one but I was a needle in a Vancouver haystack. While she was undercover, she found mom who got killed and Terry rescued me. She took me home and we've hung out together ever since."

"Wow!"

"Oh, and in the states, I made a poem that made me a bundle, got me on the bad side of the Disciples and they shot me at the big convention. Terry got Bill Page."

She pointed at the spot where the bullet went.

Des was flabbergasted. "All of that and you're only twenty?"

She shrugged. "So Des, has your life been better up here?"

He looked hesitant. "My previous life was very sad. Both my wife and daughter passed away. I fell on hard times, lost my job at Boeing and ended up sleeping in my car. You seem to be the only bright spot."

He winked and she smiled. They had a gentle hug.

When they stood apart she asked, "So Mr. Horse Whisperer, what's in your future?"

"Let's say this is a new life and I can't imagine going back."

"Your happy place, as they say."

He nodded. "I take it you are headed home after this."

"Yes. I'll be going back to my home and schooling in London England when this is all wrapped up."

Des looked nervous. "Will this get finished, bad guys to jail and good guys win?"

She shrugged. "It's never over until it's over. We'll have to wait and see."

Des looked at the dust following an official car. "Looks like the sheriff's back."

They watched as Sheriff Abe calmly shuffled over the plowed field humps eventually reaching them. He smiled. "Your aunt told me to tell you to come to town. She's got everyone smoothed over and needs you."

Jess was suspicious. "Do I have to go?"

"Suit yourself. I'm just doing as I'm told. Coming or not?"

She scowled at him, arms folded and shook her head.

"I'll pass on the news," and he turned away.

Jess looked at Des. Suddenly the sheriff turned on her, pointed a taser at her and his gun at Des. "Surprise!"

Everything went blank.

She woke up in a stinky factory room of some kind. Her hands and feet were cuffed together in a closet or janitor room.

What next?

---

INWARDLY TERRY'S HEART POUNDED, and she broke into a sweat. She thought she was doomed. Her stand-off choice wasn't something she looked forward to. It would have left an embittered Milton Hobson alive to wreak vengeance.

But she would escape to fight another day.

She looked ahead at the guard holding the door open for her. Looking left and right, feeling the cool grass under her stocking feet, she went across the exquisitely manicured berm estate. Ignoring her car, she disappeared into the woods.

Terry wondered how many bombs and bugs they'd installed in her car and probably her shoes and purse while she met Hobson. Best abandon it.

Ciao Milton.

---

THE TWO SECURITY guards watched in surprise as Terry Reid disappeared into the woods in her sock feet.

"She knows we have her shoes, right? Never even asked for them."

"Yeah, Milton's goons probably put bugs and spikes in them, anyway," said James.

"What about her car? She walked right past it."

"I saw some guys fooling with it."

"Booby traps and trackers?"

"No doubt," agreed James.

"I got a text. Says, 'Take the car away'."

James leaned into Ben's ear and whispered, "You can try and start it, if you want."

"Not a chance!"

---

"Hɪ Rɪᴄᴋ. Call off the big Kaboom," Terry said on her phone. "Milton let me go."

"I'm not sure I have something to pull a big Kaboom, anyway. Got some bad news."

"What?"

Rick hesitated to answer her. "The sheriff grabbed Jess."

Terry stood in momentary panic, speechless.

"Terry? You there?"

"Yes. How'd you find out?"

"Somehow Des got a message to me. He said I was the only one he could trust after the parade thing. Abe walked up, tasered her, wacked him on the head, left him."

*Ransom or vengeance?*

"Any idea where they went?"

"Alaska's a big place."

Terry stood, scrambling her brains, thinking. Where the hell have they taken Jess?

"Can you call Abe and convince him to come meet you some-where…secluded. I'm assuming if he hasn't tried to contact me, he has other plans for her."

"Are you looking for something like a cliff overlooking a raging river for his quiz?"

"Sounds fine."

"Where are you, Terry?"

"Outskirts of town...93 street near Jenkins Park, in my sock feet."

"I have Joyce here and she'll come fetch you and take you to the meeting place with Abe."

SHERIFF ABE WAS HEADED for the office when his personal phone rang.

Rick. Uh-oh. "Hey Rick. What's up?"

"Abe. We gotta talk. Can we meet?"

"Why should I do that?" Abe asked suspiciously.

"I went in your office and noticed you had the FBI Agent tied up. It was a good chance to get her computer, your computer and all the files I could grab."

*Oh my God!* "So what?"

"Those World Oil knobs must have some money to buy this back or would you rather I sent it all to the New York Times?"

Gulp.

"Meet me at Kelvin's Reach in thirty minutes. Come alone and unarmed with a bag of cash."

Click.

Abe swung his car around and headed for the Reach. He'd smooth him over then push him over the cliff. The river will have him in the Beaufort Sea in three days.

Goodbye to that pain in the ass, Rick. He parked his car a mile away, ditched the uniform and clunky weapons belt donning familiar camouflage. Not quite the same color as the stuff he used in Afghanistan but comfy and effective. Pity he didn't have a sniper rifle. Big old slow Rick won't be hard to find.

It was a nice day as he melted into the cover of the forest. He had to admit packing a nine-millimeter pistol was much lighter than a sniper rifle, scope and glasses. The birds chirped in the bushes all around him as he worked his way up to the Reach. Rumour had it that's where Rick pushed off wife number four.

He might just ask him about it before giving him a shove. It would make a good background story for later.

A cold metal gun barrel gently pushed behind his ear while a knife jabbed his lower back. His gun, phone and knife were yanked from him.

Rough hands zipped his hands behind his back then propelled him forward to the edge of the Reach.

It was a long way down into a boiling river.

"We need to talk Abe or whatever your name is," said a cold, female voice.

Suddenly he was rammed face-down in the moss-covered rock. The end for him?

"What's your phone code?"

He laid in sullen silence.

She pulled him to his feet and pushed him further along.

Terry backed him to the edge of the Reach, a cliff dropping two hundred and twelve feet into the boiling Sandford River. Lovers leap.

"Where's Jess?" said Terry, eyes slits, face angry.

Abe grinned. "Tell you and you push me off? What's the sport in that?"

"Sport? You worked with the McIlhennys in Afghanistan shooting innocent people."

He spat on the rock at his feet. "No innocents over there! Killing fields."

"The perfect place for serial killers like you."

"Yeah, so."

"Jess."

"Let me loose and we'll talk. Don't and maybe I'll jump on my own and you'll never know."

Terry hesitated.

"You didn't get a ransom call because they aren't doing a trade. This is retribution for all the times you screwed over the Disciples."

A look of rage passed her face. "What's the code for your phone?"

"Undo my hands and I'll tell you."

She put the gun in her pocket and dug out the phone she took from him with her right hand. Her left hand wielded the nasty looking knife, her preferred weapon.

"Code!"

"Let me pop these zip ties and I'll show you."

———

ABE TOOK A CALCULATED RISK. He was desperate. She seemed enraged and angry, both causing her logic impairment. He had five seconds tops to pull this off.

He slowly bent over toward her, his hands zipped behind his back. Her knife and face didn't move. Pulling his shoulders forward and yanking his wrists on his butt he felt the plastic zips cut his skin and suddenly snap. Arms were free.

Like lightning his hand lashed out grabbing her knife hand while his other grabbed her phone hand. He saw she was a right hander and would never drop the phone, her only connection to Jess.

Abe stood, his hands grappling hers, his back to the Reach. With any luck at all he could wrestle her around and over the cliff. He heard a boom, which he thought was thunder, then found himself getting weak, dropping his hands.

He watched her face as she lifted a right leg up and kicked him backwards into the boiling torrent.

———

TERRY WATCHED Abe fall for what seemed like minutes, landing in the froth and wild water. A camouflaged figure came out of the nearby bush with a scoped sporting rifle.

They both stood, looking down.

"Nice shot, Rick."

"Thank you. I wondered if Abe was bringing anyone else with him. Good insurance."

"Yes."

"Blackheart."

"What?" she asked.

"His phone code. Abe was clearly an ex-Army sniper that liked his job too much. I watched him use his code. He thought it was a cool name."

"He was one of the McIlhennys outfit, sniper group in Afghanistan. They liked their job so much the Disciples hired them."

"I could see he was smooth, but something was broken inside."

Terry read the phone messages and texts, then took a big breath. "Can you drive me to a pizza joint and a used clothing store?"

"What?"

---

HARRY AND KEN sat at the security consul, bored and tired. Normally they'd take turns dozing off, but Randolph Hobson was sleeping in his top story suite, again, tonight. He'd fire their asses in a heartbeat if he caught either of them with so much as a droopy eyelid.

Their security consul swept every floor, even the washrooms, with video cameras. World Oil spent almost a million dollars for the technology to get rid of two union employees and they made sure the remaining two didn't go for food or bathroom breaks, either.

It was a year ago, World Oil installed a Security Management System (SMS) computer program that sent them over a planned route in a prescribed amount of time. The time automatically became shorter as all the guards used the routes the computer told them. Breaks were frowned upon and cost them valuable time.

The 'SMS' was an adaptation of their warehouse forklift program designed to speed up production and reduce manpower. World Oil deemed the reduced cost per load outweighed that of workplace accidents which skyrocketed.

Survival of the fittest but not the smartest.

The times of the eight guards were posted on a list for them all to see. The older, slower guards were weeded out and fired leaving only

Ken and Harry, the youngest and fastest with the largest bladders and eating the least. The last two survivors could travel every inch of the building but see or notice nothing.

It was two o'clock in the morning and both arrived at the main control console at the entrance for their fifteen-minute dinner break. Neither had thought to bring food as they feared for their jobs. Showing up with a lunch kit sent the message they were going to sit down, eat, and take up valuable time.

They looked up when they heard someone tapping on the front door glass. A person with a company shirt, thick glasses, hat around her ears, building pass hanging around her neck and a large pizza box. Suspicious, Harry nodded to Ken who went to the door to investigate.

Mmm...pizza!

"What?" he asked her while looking at the greasy pizza box. The label said pepperoni.

She smiled, tapped the pizza box. "Big day, tomorrow, Mr. Hobson needs some background on the refinery's cat cracker done before he wakes up. Fifteen- million-dollar item. You don't want to piss him off, do you?"

Sure as hell not.

"See my iron ring? I'm an engineer and I'm here to help," she winked. "Do you like Pizza? Thought you'd like some."

"Engineers! Alright." He pulled the door open a crack.

"Thanks!" She drove the door into Ken's face, pulled a pistol with a silencer out of the box, aimed it at the middle of Harry's chest and shot twice.

Bang...pew, pew.

She dragged the stunned guard behind the big control desk. The guard she shot now moved, groaning.

"You had your vest? Good planning or you'd be dead."

She flipped both of them over face down and zipped their wrists and feet together.

Carefully she put a thick zip tie around each of their necks. She clicked each one as tight as she dared.

"I'm not going to kill you, but these ties are very tight. If you relax, stay quiet and don't move around you can breathe just enough to stay alive."

Their rasping breathing and panicked bulging eyes was the reply.

There was a large plastic bladder of liquid in the pizza box which she threw under the control panel and shot a detonator in the middle. Poof. The liquid sprayed up into the control panel wiring and controls, bubbling and crackling.

The trussed-up guards were even more panicked than before as the liquid splashed on them.

"Just a special corrosive salt-brine, boys. Table salt and water. There won't be a wire or circuit board left in fifteen minutes.

She glanced at the fading monitors and knew these were the only guards. Milton had kindly given her a building tour earlier that day. There was a service elevator to the top, at the end of the hall.

---

IN THE BUILDING'S PENTHOUSE, World Oil CEO Randolph Hobson settled into his hand-made fifty-six-thousand-dollar bed covered with nineteen-thousand-dollar sheets and an eleven-thousand-dollar pillow. His silk pajamas, a gift from the King of England crackled with static sparks. These fricking pajamas are itchy. Hate them all.

I need some sleep.

His brother Milton ordered him to be here, ready for the big purchase tomorrow bright and early. His mind roamed to the two point six-billion-dollar refinery purchase. Old tired iron but a money maker. Pre-pollution regulations, non-union and runs on discount Alberta crude from his own Fort Mac operation so it's all good. It'll be good to sign on the dotted line after giving them a scare about closing the place, of course. Sheeple are good for business.

Ironically, he dreamt of sheep.

*Pew!*

What was that?

He woke in the dark with a start at the sound of a 'pew' and a crunch. Rolling to the side, his left hand aimed for the bedside lamp, his right fumbled to raise his eye covers.

What's that burning smell?

He successfully turned his light on, uncovered his eyes and found a pistol with a sizzling hot silencer very close to his cheek. His eyes followed the gun to an arm and up to a stern face sitting in a chair beside him. His entry door was swinging open, lock broken.

A cold voice asked tonelessly, "Good evening Mr. Hobson. Can I call you Randy?"

He sat up and put on his glasses and looked at the person with the gun. It was a woman. "You're the one with the gun. Call me whatever you want."

The gun wielder said nothing.

"Who are you?" he sputtered.

She had the silenced pistol at his face. "Terry Reid. Tell me where Jess is or I'll fill you full of bullet holes starting with your feet and work my way up."

He took a few moments to get over the shock. "Humph. My people will be here in an instant."

She made a face. "I'd doubt it. Their fighting for breath as we speak. Where's Jess!"

Randolph looked nervous. "Why would I know about this Jess person?"

"Because you and your brother Milton run the Disciples, that's why. Speak up while you can." She shoved the hot pistol into his cheek.

"Oow. You're as good as dead!" he gasped, immediately regretting his bravado.

"I don't have a lot of time which means you don't either."

She jumped up, landing on him with her knees and elbows. Blows rained down on him from everywhere. Then he was flipped over face-down and felt his arms bent behind him and his wrist tied together. He was ready to cry out when something gripped his throat tightly.

It slowly clicked as it got tighter. Hard to breathe.

"Feel that around your throat? A little a skill I picked up in Syria, one of your oil producing hell holes. While you made a few billion I picked up this torture trick." Randolph strained for breath. The woman sat on his back giving him instructions. "Your guards downstairs are getting the same treatment. Only two guards? World Oil is so cheap."

He laid there in petrified silence.

"The way this works is I ask you a question and you give me the answer. If not, I click this throat tie a little tighter. If you relax you can breathe. Panic and you're dead. Get it?"

He laid like a stone and rasped, "Yes."

"Where's Jess?"

"I… don't… know…" he gasped.

He felt the nylon around his throat click a notch, almost too much.

"I have so much patience and there's only a couple more clicks and we're done. Get it?"

It was all he could do to barely breathe. "…ya…"

"This isn't working for us, is it? We could speed this up with that plastic bag with 'World Oil on the sides. Hold still and I'll go get it." She was back. "You are the only company in the world still polluting the world with shitty plastic bags and you might die with one on your head. Imagine the pictures and headlines, Randolph?"

He felt his head being pulled back by his hair and the clammy plastic back sliding over his head. Darkness. A pair of hands secured it around his neck. The bag sucked closer to his face with each desperate breath.

"It'll take about twenty seconds and you'll be trying to inhale this bag. I'll count you down. If you change your mind lift your right leg up and down a couple of times."

He only saw blackness. The plastic clung to his face, getting tighter and tighter. It didn't help he was claustrophobic. He heard the count down through the thin bag.

The plastic was sucking into his mouth and throat. Was his silence worth his life? All those lives? Now the young Poem Girl's life? What had he done?

There was no end to the butchery and madness he'd been involved with.

"Twenty, nineteen, eighteen…"

Randolph felt the plastic back in his mouth and almost gagged. No air. With the last of his strength he feebly raised and lowered his leg twice. Did this mad woman see it?

"So, let's hear what you have to say Mr. Hobson."

The bag was yanked off his head and he could breathe despite the throat tie. The cool air felt heavenly. He could have sobbed—if he could have sucked in a lungful of air…

"Speak!" she commanded impatiently, opening the throat tie a couple of clicks.

He rasped like his life depended on it. "It… it was Milton's idea to get into this Disciples business. He had a connection to that idiot President Jackson and his Revisionist schemes. 'Make it an American world, ours for the taking.'"

"Jess!"

"Milton always thought her poem woke the people against us. He has her in his Akme Blending plant… soap!"

"Akme… soap? Why there?"

"No security and it has…sodium hydroxide."

"Why?"

"It's… also known as Drano. Dissolves everything."

Terry sat back and looked at Randolph with killer eyes. She was angrier than she could remember, barely holding back the urge to pull out her knife and rip his guts out.

"Don't kill me! I did as you asked."

She said nothing for a full minute then pulled her knife and moved it to menace his face. Then she slid the blade to his throat and gingerly cut the tie choking his throat and then cut his wrist ties.

Randolph started crying with relief.

"Get up and get dressed. You have one minute then we are leaving, or you'll be going through that window and down to the street."

Despite his pain Randolph jumped from his bed, dropping his pajamas as he threw on clothes like this was the contest of his life with the angriest person he had ever met aiming a gun at his belly. He dressed faster than any fireman.

She looked like she hoped he'd be late.

"You'd better have car keys for something in your parking lot."

"Yes! Yes, I do! Right here." Randolph nodded as he hopped into shoes with socks barely slid on.

"Out!"

He looked down at her hand, carrying a bottle of his most expensive Cognac. Terry took a pearl lighter from his nearby gold-plated ashtray and lit his pillow on fire.

"Service elevator!"

As she shoved him through the door, she smashed the over-proof bottle on the thick carpeted floor which burst into flame from the pillow. It spread quickly. The damaged entrance control station ensured it would go unnoticed for a while.

There were a couple of dozen more bottles stored in the room to add fuel to the fire. By the time they got in the car and headed out the alcohol would go up along with the synthetic carpeting and everything else.

She really looked like she was eager to do those terrible things. "Got wallet, car keys, ID?"

Randolph was chilled, resisting the urge to urinate in his pants. "Yes!"

As they went down in the elevator, she aimed her gun in his back. "Sprinklers in this place?"

"Ah, no."

"I thought so, you're so cheap."

"Why?"

"They're going to think you were burnt alive and there's nothing left of you."

The elevators opened and she carefully surveyed the cars. Nobody. "Which vehicle?"

Randolph fumbled with the keys in his pocket. "Over there…that Beemer."

"Take me to that soap factory. Take whatever ID you need. One peep from you and I'll cut your balls off then stab you in the spine."

He nodded.

"You drive. I'm beside you. No funny stuff. Go to that factory at a normal safe speed. No cops."

Randolph nodded his sweaty face. "I don't drive much."

"Today's your day to learn."

Terry scanned the area as he drove from the lot. The automatic barrier knew the chip in his car and opened up without pause. It was two-thirty in the morning, so the streets were quiet.

She imagined the fire in his room was very intense by now, bottles of alcohol exploding and adding to the flames. She'd closed the door to ensure a very hot room. Hopefully this would be a distraction.

"What do you plan to do with me?"

"Plan? You just plan to keep yourself alive, buddy and we'll see what happens."

---

MILTON SAW the text confirmation from Randolph the poem girl was hidden in the soap factory.

Perfect.

He then called and ordered the factory security to leave the place. Nobody breaks into a stinky, dangerous soap factory, especially with a witch's brew of boiling lye and other dangerous liquids.

# 18

## DRIVING A MAD-WOMAN

Milton had dinner with his family as per his usual routine. Afterwards he excused himself to go back to the office to get ready for the big refinery sale, tomorrow.

A decent alibi if someone should wonder where the poem girl went, if it should ever point in his direction but this would be the perfect crime.

It wasn't the first time he'd personally made someone disappear. He found murder something of a logical challenge.

RANDOLPH TRIED to keep the situation out of his mind and drove. Should have brought his driving glasses.

She watched him carefully as he drove the deserted streets towards the soap plant.

"I've been hunting you psychos for years. Seen a lot of people die along the way. Good, decent, God fearing folks. Are you and Milton both psychopaths?"

Randolph gasped and sputtered. "N-n-no! Never! I just went along. Milton was the brains. I've never personally killed anyone."

"So, you were just the flunky like the guards for the Gestapo?"

He said nothing as he steered around a corner. "Yes, you could say I was a stooge all along. I tried to ignore what he was doing, pretending it was all good. I passed bullets to the murderer while turning the other way."

"The Psycho and the stooge with way too much money?"

He said nothing because she was right.

"Slow down, Randy. An auto barrier?"

"Yes. The plant is deserted at night except for a couple of security guys."

"Which your brother dismissed, no doubt. Turn your headlights out."

The barrier opened with the car electronic chip and they continued on the lane.

"Stop here."

"Here? This is the middle of the lane."

"Do it!"

---

SHE KNEW there would be a video cam on the lot and entrance but not on the roadway.

"Out!" she commanded. "Lead me to her."

They entered the factory through a side door and stepped along the walkway between the rows of huge vats interconnected with miles of pipe.

A multimillion-dollar maze for a bar of soap.

---

MILTON HOBSON FELT the tinny clunk when his truck door shut. Before he turned the ignition key, a beep on his phone got his attention. It was Fred, their most trusted legal supervisor.

*"Randolph wants to split the company and run – Fred."*

So, Randolph was getting cold feet when he had to help eliminate someone, was he? I should have taken the signs more seriously. He's been trying to distance himself since we came to Alaska. Coward!

*"The HQ building is burning to the ground. Randolph is unaccounted for. – Fred"*

A split of this magnitude would cost billions. Unfortunate facts and evidence of their Disciples operations would come to light. The Council wouldn't appreciate that.

The Randolph gone part? Handy.

He flopped open the trucks glove compartment and dug out the lovely little Colt revolver he kept there. Old school but bumps them off and keeps the brass.

Milton quelled his panicked thoughts and drove to the soap factory in a leisurely, law abiding fashion, using his unremarkable pickup truck. World Oil had dozens, all identical. He drove through the auto gate and parked at the very back, hidden with a stack of pallets and some rusty barrels. No cameras.

Going through the door with his ID card he strolled confidently towards the narrow grip mesh-decked cat walks. After a few steps he was at the level of the tops of the big vats. The guard rails were just wide enough apart for his passage.

He confidently strolled towards the huge stainless steel, glass-lined cauldrons. After climbing the various walkways, he located the one he sought...the container of Sodium Hydroxide, also known as Drano. Perhaps he could coax Randolph down here and inspect the soap factory one more time.

Milton Hobson was an engineer by profession. He saw the giant vat was cool. Weekend. He stood on the catwalk, unhooked the safety chain on the rail and leaned down to the big handle marked Danger. He pulled the handle to Open and tilted the six-foot-wide lid on its hinge. Assisting springs helped easily moved it right exposing the cool liquid.

The heat, chemicals in the air and effort turned him into a ball of sweat which ran into his eyes and down his shirt. His glasses became so steamed up he could barely see anything. Nearby he spotted the little electronic control booth, air filtered and air conditioned. It was the perfect place to cool off.

He wasn't a young man anymore.

Milton stood in relief, leaning over to the waist level cold air fans. It felt glorious. He slid down and sat on the floor drinking in the cold air.

What was that clumping noise coming along the catwalk? He peaked up to peer through the glass window to see brother Randolph coming towards him.

Randolph wasn't dead after all? This could be a tidy way to be rid of him. He was surely having second thoughts about being a Disciple, anyway. Fool.

Milton dug his pistol from his pocket. Every once in a while, everyone failed him, and he was forced to take matters into his own hands. Nothing personal. Comes with the global territory.

Using his handkerchief, he cleaned his glasses. Squinting towards Randolph he spied someone following him closely behind. Could it be that meddler Terry Reid?

Maybe he could make a more interesting offer this time. Go along with it or both die.

He liked the odds of this one.

RANDOLPH WAS TERRIFIED, leading Terry Reid to Jess in the control room. Hopefully she was where he left her hours ago. A voice called in his ear while a gun barrel jabbed his back. "Where are we going?" his captor snarled.

He paused and leaned back to Reid. "We go past here to get to Jess."

The gun barrel stopped poking his back which he took as an okay and he resumed his mission.

They both climbed the steel mesh stairs and the narrow catwalk along the tops of the huge vats. They'd been turned off since Friday but held heat for days afterward. It was stinky and brutally hot. Passing a tall booth on his right, his heart jumped into his throat when the door opened and Milton stood before him, aiming a gun at his midsection.

"Stop!" Milton commanded. "If you want Jess.

Terry's gun pointed back at him.

At the end of a deadly line.

He was standing between two desperate people, both aiming their weapons him to get to the enemy on the other side.

---

TERRY WAS FORCED to aim her pistol at Milton through Randolph. This narrow catwalk made any dash forward impossible. A standoff. She couldn't guarantee a killing shot on Milton, especially if Randolph pitched in. Even if he ran, he'd be in the way. She decided to push them a little. "Where's Jess, you jerks! I'm getting impatient."

Milton looked past Randolph, both eyes on Terry. "I'll show you where she is and we can all go home, if you side with us."

"Out of the way boys," she warned.

"You won't easily get by us, Ms. Reid. My brother will work quite well as a shield. Your shooting may fail, and Jess will be left all alone to her fate so listen to my proposition before you start shooting and bullets are ricocheting uncontrolled off this metal decking."

She stood silent, pointing her weapon.

"Drop your gun first, Reid. Put it on the floor and I'll make you an offer you can't refuse. Both you and Jess will go free."

Terry saw there was an opening in the guard rail, but it led to the yawning vat of Drano. Randolph wasn't going to step forward and stand beside it and Milton wouldn't let him. She'd have to hope an opportunity presented itself.

Milton shouted, "Smell that? Burns your nostrils doesn't it? Sodium hydroxide... dissolves everything, especially when they heat it up Monday morning. There won't be a bit of skin and bone left. Even your fillings will be gone."

Randolph looked at Milton nervously. "This is murder!"

Milton pointed his gun in Randolph's face. "You idiot! This is high stakes, not a parlour game."

"Your Disciples have killed hundreds if not thousands," added Terry, hoping to fuel this spat.

"She's right," Milton scoffed. "And you need to find a body to make a case. You, dear brother, were already incinerated in your apartment fire set by this damned Reid woman. You're already dead."

"No!"

"Shut up! Drop that gun Reid or you'll never see Jess again. Right now."

Terry thought hard before putting it down. She had the option of jumping behind Randolph, who was a fair size, but not now.

Milton was looking deranged. "Get over by the rail near the vat, Randolph. Go!"

RANDOLPH STOOD up to his full six-foot four-inch height. He knew he was doomed in any case, especially now that Milton knew they were splitting World Oil. Could there be something he could do to save the Poem Girl?

Distracting Milton might help Terry.

"Why do you hate me Milton?" he pleaded waving his hands.

"Hate you?" Milton shrugged. "I've built this operation from nothing while you came along for the ride. I did all the dirty work. And now I hear you want to take my money and run."

"Your money? It's inherited money for both of us."

"I built it from millions to billions!"

"Milton, you always were such a drama queen," Randolph grinned, giving him a finger in defiance. "I know you made my family...disappear." Why not? He was doomed and knew it.

It was inevitable. His grin faded as Milton grimly raised his pistol and aimed, eyes bulging in concentration. There was a bang. Randolph felt the bullet thud into his chest. As his legs crumpled beneath him, Randolph felt a knife fly past his hair. He didn't see it continue past and stab into Milton's throat.

Fleetingly, Randolph wondered what Hell was going to look like as he toppled forward into blackness. He knew his brother would be joining him.

---

TERRY STOOD beside Randolph as Milton aimed his gun at them. She wondered which one of them Milton hated more. They'd find out, shortly. She had no gun, but her knife nestled in its hiding place like a viper. She watched as he raised the pistol, waving back and forth. Who's first? He moved to Randolph and pulled the trigger.

Brotherly love?

As Randolph dropped, Terry's knife flashed in the dim light, catching Milton in the throat. He stared at her, knowing he had seconds to live while his gun hit the metal deck.

It didn't take her long to heave Randolph, then Milton into the steaming vat. It took Terry a minute to figure out how to lock the lid of the vat down. Perfect.

Goodbye Disciples Duo.

No body, no case. Her old mentor Montreal mafia Bob would be pleased at her imagination.

---

JESS WAS TIED up and couldn't move. Her mouth was taped shut. Milton used actual hand cuffs so she couldn't break them like Terry had showed her she could have if they were ties. It bugged her she was the bait to trap Terry.

Her attempts to find her father had dragged Terry into a wild goose chase. She'd stupidly got grabbed by the sheriff and here she was, hoping Terry didn't die. The thought crumbled her to tears.

---

TERRY RAN from the Drano vats area desperately searching for Jess. She wouldn't have been hidden in plain sight, so she had to be in a control room, workshop or a closet. This plant was a maze.

Where would he put her? He was an engineer who thrived on efficiency. It would be handy over clever. Close to the vat, well-lit with communications. A control room!

She glanced around watching for windows. There it was in the center of the soap plant, central to the control of the operation. Two flights of stairs and she was at the door. Gun at the ready she kicked the door open and hit the floor listening and watching. Something made a noise behind a janitor closet door.

Terry flipped the lights on, tiptoed to the door, yanking it open.

Jess!

---

TERRY! Jess couldn't remember the last time she was so happy. She mumbled behind the tape on her face and squirmed for joy as she sat on the floor.

Her aunt sat down beside her and hugged her hard. She grabbed a side of the tape on her mouth. "Sorry kid." The tape was removed in a painful flash.

"Ouch! Hi Aunty. I'm so sorry I got you into this. Milton grabbed me as a hostage and I couldn't do anything about it!" she sobbed.

Terry got to work picking the hand cuff locks. "It's okay Jess. The Hobsons are gone."

Jess creakily stood up and hugged Terry for a long minute.

"Are they really gone?"

"Gone! They will be making the world a cleaner place, bless them."

---

THEY SAT around the living room at Rick Forest's home. The stories came and went fast and furious. It had been an eventful time for them all.

215

Jess cleared her throat, and the group went silent. "I think Aunt Terry has something to say to you all, don't you?"

Terry put her coffee down, looking surprised. "Oh, I suppose I do. This was a wild time for us and each of you helped pull all this together and stopped the Alaskan takeover.

"Joyce. Thanks for sleuthing out the background details on how the Milton plan was supposed to come together.

"Rick. Your drone strike on the pipeline controls gave us valuable leverage and distraction. Sorry about destroying your drone."

He grinned. "I got it paid for by someone in the Pentagon! Friends in low places."

Terry continued, "Well done. Dean, Trev and Dan. You managed to get the community guard people stopped and neutralized before they got to town and without anyone getting hurt.

"Des. You got your community friends to distract the National Guards in the nick of time. "

Rick's wife interrupted her. "Terry there's a General Brant on the phone for you. He said you'd know who he was."

"The president!" blurted Joyce. "You should probably get that."

Terry was already out of her chair and heading for the kitchen phone. The receiver was shaped like a cow horn. A vet's house, alright.

She cleared her throat. "Terry Reid speaking."

---

GENERAL BRANT'S secretary managed to hunt down the phone number and dialed it while the General patiently waited. So many events had just taken place and it all worked out well. He shuddered to think of what could have happened if the Disciples had taken over Alaska.

"Terry Reid speaking."

"Major! This is General Brant speaking. How are you?"

"Fine, sir."

"Thank you for stopping the Alaska Disciples. We thought there was some funny business with World Oil and those communities. You connected the dots and stopped their plan."

"Jess and I were already here on another errand, sir. We just went along with it."

"That's an understatement. So, you were there, already?"

"Yes. Jess thought her dad was here in one of the communities, so we came to look."

"Did she find him?"

"Yes, she did. It turns out we were together picking rocks in a field with him the whole time. It's a wacky world."

Brant added "I'll say."

"What happens to the community folks, sir?"

"We've decided they've innocently been misled. The people pulling the strings will be gone and the citizens are welcome to stay to pursue farms and mineral rights as before. They're council will give us a plan going forward and we'll monitor it from there."

"But no National Guard..."

"You can probably smell their uniforms burning as we speak."

"Good call."

"I'll let you go Major. Again, you've saved our bacon and we do appreciate it."

"Thank you, sir."

THE GENERAL HUNG UP, deep in thought about the Alaska incident. He hoped the story could be kept quiet for a while to prevent copy-cat incidents from the various militias, state-side. Perturbed by these thoughts General Brant dialed a very private number. A voice answered.

"Joint Chief of staff, Admiral Lowry speaking."

"Norm! How's it going? Brant here."

"Afternoon General! What can I do for you?"

"Norm! This Alaska Disciples thing...do we have troops up there, finally?"

"Yes sir. A force of twelve hundred arrived by plane, yesterday."

"Plane? How did you do that?"

"We contracted Sandros Hammar Corp. to do it. He had some big planes, filled it with some knockout gas so the troops were sleeping and flew them with his robot special GPS control system...or were they robots?"

"That's clever. Why didn't we think of that?"

"It's all his proprietary special tech. We can't get close to it."

"How were our troops when they got to Alaska?"

"Shaky. It was like the biggest hangover, ever, but they are coming around."

"Where'd they land?"

"We had a few dependable men who filled the trenches on the runways just before the planes arrived. There were a few rough dirt strips we commandeered, as well."

"And when they needed to land, Hammar's GPS did the rest without the special lights and such?"

"Correct."

"Come Norm, why can't we buy that tech or appropriate it for the US military?" the general asked pointedly, to make Admiral Lowry squirm in his chair.

"There are a few reasons sir. We can't afford it, we couldn't maintain it and if we just took it, he could shut off the remaining tech he looks after for us like missiles, bombs, spaceships and satellites etc. etc."

"So he has us under his heel?"

"Very much so. He's very powerful."

"Dammit. Let's move on. The Disciple captives are going to be housed...where?" *Especially former Governor Fairfield!*

"Attu Island, again. Their new camp will be on the other side of the island from the old burnt out prison area."

"Ah. The prison camp that the submarine missiles blew to bits?"

"Yes."

"Did you ever find out who did that to Attu and the old Disciples camp, Norm?"

"Not conclusively, sir. All we have are a few grainy satellite shots on the misty day. Missile subs are fairly common."

Brant paused. "Nobody will admit to it?"

"No sir."

"Could this mysterious attack be the same as who had the Verbeelding plant bombed out?"

"No sir. There was no connection with the Verbeelding factory bombings in Vietnam. We do know that."

Brant's stopped breathing for a few seconds. "Well, who did it? Who bombed Attu Island?"

"Apparently, according to our sources it appears to be…"

"Dammit, out with it, Norm! I'm going to have a heart attack here!"

"We are quite sure it was …Sandros Hammar."

# A NOTE FROM THE AUTHOR

Thank you for reading yet another exciting chapter in the adventures of Theresa Reid and her clever niece, Jessica Reid.

My little yarn takes place closer to my home than you might imagine. The incidents are truer than you think. This merry band of commune dwellers is loosely based on real events with the names and location changed.

Let your imagination run wild and do a bit of searching on the magic internet and see if you can find out for yourself but I didn't suggest it if anyone asks.

You will recognize a few recurring characters such as Dean, Trev and Gomez from *His Disciples Watch* and Gina Gospel's name from '*His Disciples Deceive*' and Amelia, Gulinda, and General Brant from '*His Disciples Replicate*'.

Major Reid runs with a fast crowd.

In closing, we are in nervous, uncertain times. As Dr. Bonnie Henry, our BC Chief Medical officer says, 'Be kind, be calm, be safe.' Wise words.

Pull together like Terry and Jess. Help is coming,

*Patrick D. Ferris*

# EXCERPT FROM HIS DISCIPLES
## PROPHECY OF DOOM

Patrick D. Ferris
*Coming in 2021:*

The sun smiled down, the birds sang on the green expanse of mani-cured grass, and massive fountain centrepiece, all maintained on the taxpayers' dollar. Nearby, the wide marble steps were built to welcome people to the building's entrance and was crowded with humanity, on guard and full of armed menace.

An insurrection.

The stern men proudly stood, feeling like armed mercenaries of old, menacing but without the danger. They were paid to intimidate. Pocket money for the grocery clerks, car salesman and truck drivers to pay for their home weaponry.

Their angry eyes glowered down at the deserted lawn and foun-tain, empty except for a single defiant person. One cloaked figure slouched against the massive concrete fountain in the middle of the State Building yard. Its hands were in its front pocket, hood hiding its head. It stood, disinterested.

The Reaper had been motionless for hours.

The leader of the armed men, Ed, shuddered thinking the dark cloaked figure looked like the Grim Reaper. It made him hold his rifle tighter.

Ed Bass and a hundred bearded, stocky men crowded the steps of the Michigan State Legislature bearing pistols sticking out of holders, exotic assault rifles and homemade protest signs, some misspelt or insensible.

Ed dressed like the others clad in dark or camouflage long sleeve clothing, mostly on sale from Wal-Mart, as defense against the morning chill. All had work gloves to keep fingers warm while clutching their cold AR's and AK's pointed to the ground like they saw Delta Forces on television stalking Iraq or Afghanistan. Ed and his men had never been there, thankfully, but liked to look the part.

Image was everything.

Invincibles among the innocents.

The Grim Reaper watching them made him nervous but he kept such negative thoughts to himself. They stood in silence, cold, hungry, legs tired and many needing a bathroom break. Tight ranks kept them warm.

The State office wouldn't let them in to use the toilets.

Without warning 'The Reaper' sprinted into them like lightning, extending evil black batons from each hand, slashed their faces and hands before they could utter a sound. They were huddled together so tightly nobody dared shoot.

The Reaper split Ed's group like the blade of an ax with its elbows and batons flying, mowing them down like spindly sunflowers. Something smashed Ed's face, crushing his nose and his eye but he watched, frozen, as black bats beat them like whips as they screamed, blood pouring and bones breaking, dropping their guns, stampeding over their companions to escape. He saw them dissolve into panic and chaos. The bulls trampled each other.

Ed found himself on his back, looking at the top of the steps at the

Grim Reaper. He was going to die. For a second it dropped its hood, looked his way as the screaming crowd evaporated. It turned and disappeared into the main entrance door.

It was a woman!

---

Guard Ryan looked out the window from his security post in the state building. He was annoyed at the grim group of blockaders standing on the steps in front of him. It bugged him they were expensively armed while trying to look like the Delta's or Seals on TV. Jerk wannabes.

His good hand touched his scarred hand reminding him of his time in Afghanistan. He'd lost a lot of friends and knew the difference between soldiers and rent-a-goons. These were flabby draft dodging pretenders. He had the door locked and would die before letting them in to use the bathrooms.

Crap yourselves for all I care. His last stand over a roll of toilet paper.

The figure at the fountain intrigued him. Grim Reaper outfit? It's been there for hours looking right at the blockaders. What's its game?

As if anticipating his thoughts, the Reaper leaped forward, producing long black batons in each hand, slashing its way through the goons, making its way up the steps towards him. It reminded him of an old pirate movie with the star attacking and scattering packed sailors like a fox panics a flock of pheasants. The Reaper blew through them leaving a swath of stunned and injured men in its wake.

He grinned as the burly men screamed and ran, toppling each other over as the buccaneer slashed its way through them and made its way to his door.

'Should I let it in or shoot it?' he mumbled to himself, impressed.

The Reaper now stood in front of his door and pulled down its hood. It looked behind it then turned to him, wild cat-like eyes glaring at him expecting the door to be opened, instantly.

Ryan pulled the door wide open and made a little bow. "Major Reid! We were told you may be coming."

More coming in spring of 2021!

ALSO BY PATRICK D FERRIS


Larry and Giselle Sports Romance Series

A Gypsy Romance

A Gypsy Engagement

A Gypsy Haunting


*Terry Reid Mysteries*

His Disciples Watch

His Disciples Sleep

His Disciples Deceive

His Disciples Replicate

His Disciples in Motion


*Short Story Collection*

Fragmented Thoughts Random Directions

# ABOUT THE AUTHOR

You can contact Patrick at
www.https://patrickdferris.com

www.ingramcontent.com/pod-product-compliance
Lightning Source LLC
Chambersburg PA
CBHW060317260626
47160CB00007B/2649